Clare Connelly was raised in small-town Australia among a family of avid readers. She spent much of her childhood up a tree, Mills & Boon book in hand. Clare is married to her own real-life hero and they live in a bungalow near the sea with their two children. She is frequently found staring into space—a surefire sign she is in the world of her characters. She has a penchant for French food and ice-cold champagne, and Mills & Boon novels continue to be her favourite ever books. Writing for Modern Romance is a long-held dream. Clare can be contacted via clareconnelly.com or at her Facebook page.

Discover more at millsandboon.co.uk.

SPANIARD'S BABY OF REVENGE

CLARE CONNELLY

MILLS & BOON

First Published in Great Britain 2019
by Mills & Boon, an imprint of HarperCollins*Publishers*
1 London Bridge Street, London, SE1 9GF

© 2019 Clare Connelly

ISBN: 978-0-263-27051-8

MIX
Paper from
responsible sources
FSC® C007454

This book is produced from independently certified FSC™ paper
to ensure responsible forest management.
For more information visit www.harpercollins.co.uk/green.

Printed and bound in Spain
by CPI, Barcelona

To Esther Scott and Hunter Smith—
two of my favourite babies.

May your futures be as bright and sparkly
as all the stars in the night sky.

PROLOGUE

BENEATH HIM, MADRID sparkled like a thousand jewels, the night lights twinkling against the inky black of the sky. It was a city of history, a city rich with stories, but in that moment Antonio Herrera was conscious of only his own history.

A history that had been defined by a family feud, a hatred that was as ingrained in his heart and soul as any one man could ever have felt. Some might say that his life had been charmed, but Antonio knew the truth. Hatred for the diSalvo family ran through his Spanish blood, poisoned his mind, and he would stop at nothing to fight this war. No, to end it.

His father had been destroyed by diSalvos' machinations. A corporate empire, decades in the making, had been systematically pulled apart, and it had needed Antonio to set things to rights. At eighteen, he'd taken over the business, side-lining his father to arrest the financial bleed. He'd triaged their losses, strengthened their assets, and now, at thirty, he was a single man in charge of a billion-euro corporation, known the world over for being a titan of all types of industries.

His eyes drifted to the gleaming oak of his desk, and the file that had arrived that afternoon.

How strange the timing was. Less than a month after his father had died—a man who had been made to suffer at the hands of the diSalvos, a man Antonio would do anything for—and she had been found.

After a year of searching, a year of waiting for his elite investigator to turn over some hint of the elusive woman, and finally he had some answers.

Amelia diSalvo. Or Amelia Clifton, as she was calling herself. But a name changed nothing—she was still undeniably a diSalvo.

The missing piece of the puzzle, the woman in control of the vital shares he needed to take the jewel in the diSalvo empire into his own hands—Prim'Aqua—the shipping company that had, at one time, been owned jointly by the diSalvos and the Herreras, until both patriarchs had fallen in love with the same woman and bitterly broken their business alliance, turning friends into sworn enemies.

And now, this diminutive woman owned the shares Antonio needed, and he'd stop at nothing to convince her to sell them to him.

He stared at the photograph, looking for any resemblance to her half-brother Carlo.

There was none. Where Carlo was cast from a similar Mediterranean mould as himself, with dark hair, honeyed skin and jet-black eyes, Amelia was fair and slight.

Like her mother, he thought, remembering the world-famous supermodel who'd evidently, at one time, been the mistress of Giacomo diSalvo. Only Penny Hamilton had been tall and Amelia was tiny—as diminutive as some kind of fairy, he thought, looking at the way she was walking down the street in this photograph. It must have been a warm day, for she wore a simple cotton dress with thin straps and buttons down the front. It fell to just above her knees and the sun streamed from behind her, showing her tantalising silhouette through the dress's fine fabric.

A jolt of very masculine awareness splintered through him. Desire? For a diSalvo? How could that be, when she was part of the family that had set out to destroy his?

Regardless of his determination, his body tightened and

his eyes lingered a little longer than was necessary on the photograph, taking in the details of her pale peaches-and-cream complexion, a smile that was wide on a petite angular face, hair that was long and blonde—whether it fell naturally in those loose Botticelli curls or had been styled that morning, he would only be able to say after he'd met her in person.

And that would be soon.

In a small English village near Salisbury there was a billion-pound heiress, the daughter of a world-famous British supermodel and an Italian tycoon, a woman who'd been born into wealth and a blood rivalry. And she would be the key in winning this ancient family war.

His eyes dropped to the photograph once more. She was beautiful, but beauty was not uncommon. She was also a diSalvo, and for that he would always hate her. For one night, though, he would appeal to her sense of decency, he would implore her to return to him what should always have been his. And if she didn't, he'd find another way to secure the shares.

One way or another, he would succeed. Because he was Antonio Herrera, and failure simply wasn't an option.

CHAPTER ONE

IT HAD BEEN a perfect day. Warm and cloudless, so that the late afternoon sun filtered through the windows of her home, bathing it in a timeless golden light. But as the evening had drawn around her, the sky had clouded over and the air had begun to smell different, a portent of summer rain.

The first day of school holidays had been everything Amelia could have hoped. She'd slept late, read a book from start to finish, walked into the village for a cider at the local pub, and now she was home, making a fish pie with episodes of *The Crown* playing in the background. She'd seen the whole show already, but she loved to have the television on for company—and who better to keep company with than the Queen?

She scooped some flour from the canister in her fingertips and added it to the roux she was stirring, thickening it and breathing in the aroma gratefully—she always made a roux with garlic and saffron, and the fragrance caused her stomach to give a little groan.

Yes, the first day of school holidays had been deliciously perfect, Amelia told herself, ignoring the little pang of emptiness that pushed into her mind. It was only that a month and a half was a very long time to have off work, particularly when work was the purpose for one's life.

Teaching wasn't necessarily a calling for everyone, but it was for Amelia, and the idea of having seven whole weeks out of the classroom wasn't a prospect she entirely relished.

She'd been invited to Egypt with some of the faculty, but she'd declined. She'd done enough travelling to last a lifetime—a childhood that had seen her dragged from pillar to post depending on where her mother's latest assignment or lover had taken them, Amelia preferred to stay right where she was, in this charming village in the middle of England.

Her bluebell-shaded eyes drifted around the cottage, and a rueful half-smile touched her pink lips. It was pretty safe to say that Bumblebee Cottage was as far from the life she'd experienced as a child as possible. Her first twelve years had been spent mostly in five-star hotels, sometimes for months at a time. School had been a luxury her mother hadn't seen the necessity of, and it was only Amelia's keen desire for knowledge and the never-ending string of questions which Penny had no patience for that had led to the hiring of a tutor for Amelia.

But then Penny had died, and twelve-year-old Amelia, already so like her supermodel mother, had been shunted into another life completely. As rarefied and glamorous, but so much more public. In the wake of the supermodel's drugs-related death, Amelia had been followed everywhere she went, and her father—a man she hadn't even known about—simply hadn't been able to comprehend what life had been like for the young Amelia.

Talk about going from the frying pan and into the fire! If being the daughter of a woman like Penny Hamilton made Amelia a magnet for paparazzi, then becoming a diSalvo made her even more so.

And she'd been raised, from that moment, as a diSalvo. Loved, adored, cherished, but she couldn't outgrow the feeling that she didn't really belong.

She hadn't belonged anywhere until she'd moved to this tiny village and taken up a teaching position at Hedgecliff Academy. Unbidden, her eyes drifted to the fridge and the artwork that covered it. 'Thank you' pictures from the students she'd taught, colourful drawings with their childish swirls and squiggles—happy pictures that almost always made Amelia smile.

Fish pie finished, Amelia slipped the dish into the old Aga—it had come with the cottage and she couldn't bear to modernise the thing when it worked perfectly—and then stared around the room for a few moments. It was ridiculous to feel so lonely already.

The summer holidays had *just* begun. Only the day before she'd been surrounded by twenty-seven happy, curious eight-year-olds. Besides, she was the one who'd turned down invitations for the summer break. She had elected to stay at home.

So what good was it to dwell on the gaping void of people and company in her solitary existence? She'd chosen this life.

She'd turned her back on her father, her half-brother and the world they inhabited.

And she wouldn't have it any other way. Would she?

The cottage could not have been quainter if it had been brought to life from between the pages of a Beatrix Potter storybook. Stone, painted a pale cream, roses in the front garden, wisteria scrambling over an arch that led to the front steps and a thatched roof that showed the house to be two-storey, with little dormer windows shaped into the roof. Lights were on inside, making the cottage glow with a warmth that did something strange to Antonio's chest.

He studied it for a moment, a frown on his face as, for a brief and uncharacteristic moment, he rethought the necessity of this.

He had already bought his way into—through shell companies and entities—many of Carlo diSalvo's businesses, giving him if not a controlling interest in their operation, enough of a stake to be difficult and a nuisance to the man he had been raised to hate.

But this was different. He would gladly let the rest go if he could only get this one company under his control. And if Amelia diSalvo proved difficult, if appealing to her sense of decency didn't win her over, then he'd show her what he'd been doing and how close he was to ruining her brother.

He crossed his arms over his chest as the first drop of rain began to fall, quickly followed by another. It was a summer storm that brought with it the smell of sun-warmed grass and the threat of lightning. Inside the cottage a shape moved and he narrowed his gaze, homing in on its location.

Amelia.

He held his breath unconsciously as, with blonde hair scraped into a bun, she moved into his vision. Her face was pale; at this distance it was hard to tell, but he would say she wore no make-up. She stared out of the window for several moments and then turned away.

Certainty fired in his gut.

She was a diSalvo.

That made her fair game.

It had been less than a month since he'd buried his father and in that moment Antonio's only regret was that Javier had not lived to see this final, deeply personal revenge be enacted.

With renewed determination, his stride long and confident, he walked up the winding path. Gravel crunched underfoot and the moon peeked out from behind a storm cloud for a moment, casting him in an eerie sort of silver light. Foreboding, some might have called it, but not Antonio.

Bumblebee Cottage, a brass sign near the door proclaimed, and he ignored the image it created—of sweetness and tranquillity. Amelia diSalvo might be playing at this life, but she was the daughter of a supermodel and the most ruthless bastard on earth. And she was also the piece of the puzzle he needed—victory was within reach.

As if her loneliness had conjured a companion, the doorbell rang. Olivia wasn't so maudlin and self-indulgent to forget all common sense. It was almost nine o'clock at night—who could be calling at this hour?

She'd bought Bumblebee Cottage because of its isolation. No prying neighbours, no passing motorists—it sat nestled into a cul-de-sac of little interest to anyone but her and the farm that bordered the cottage on one side. It was a perfect, secluded bolthole. Just what she'd needed when she'd run from the life she'd found herself living.

She adored it for its seclusion but a *frisson* of something like alarm spread goosebumps over her flesh. She grabbed a meat cleaver, of all things, from the kitchen bench then moved to the door.

'Who is it?'

A man's voice answered, deep and gravelled, tinged with a European accent. 'Can you open up?'

'I can, but I'm not going to,' she muttered to herself. 'Who are you?' she called more loudly. 'What do you want?'

'Something that is easier to discuss in person.' He was hard to hear over the falling rain.

'What is it?'

'I just said—' He released a soft curse in Spanish. When she was eight, she'd mastered curse words in French, Italian, German, Spanish, Greek, Mandarin and Polish. She'd been bored on a yacht and the staff—one from each of these nationalities—had spent one late night teaching her. 'It's important, Amelia,' Antonio said.

The fact he knew her name got her attention. With a frown on her face, she unlocked the door, keeping the chain lock firmly in place so that it only cracked open a wedge.

It was dark on the porch, but enough light filtered out to show his face and it was strong and interesting.

'How do you know my name?'

There was a beat of silence and then, 'I'm a business acquaintance of your brother's. I need to speak to you.'

'Why? What about? Is it Carlo? Is he okay?'

The man's eyes flickered with something and for a moment Amelia was worried, but then he smiled. 'So far as I know, Carlo is fine. This is a proposition just for you.'

At that, Amelia frowned. 'What kind of proposition?'

His look was mysterious. 'One that is too confidential to discuss through the door.'

'It's late at night. This couldn't have waited until tomorrow?'

'I just flew in.' He shrugged, his eyes narrowing. 'Is it a bad time?'

She wanted to tell him to go away, because something about him was making her pulse fire and her heart race. Fear, surely?

'It will not take long,' he said once more, appeasing, and her eyes lifted to his.

When had she become so suspicious? True, she'd had a baptism of fire when she'd gone to live with her father and half-brother. She'd learned that there were many people out there who would hurt you—not physically, necessarily, but with any means it took. His so-called friends had proved to be wolves in couture clothing. But she'd fled those people, that world. She'd moved across the earth, to the sweetness of a tiny village, and the homeliness of Bumblebee, and she'd become not Amelia Hamilton, nor Amelia diSalvo, but Amelia Clifton—her mother's real surname. A normal name. An unrecognisable name. A name that didn't attract attention or interest, a name that was all her own.

Intrusions from her other life weren't welcome.

'Fine,' she said crisply, pushing the door shut so she could unchain it and then opening it wide.

She did a double-take. Through the one inch of open door it hadn't been possible to see exactly how handsome he was. But now? His dark hair sat straight and spiky, enhancing the sharpness of his bone structure and, rather than looking as though it had been styled that way, it was more like he'd dragged his fingers through it enough times to make the hair stand on end. His was a face that was all angles and planes, symmetrical and pleasing, with a square jaw and a chin that looked as though it had been carved from stone. Only there was a divot in its centre, as if his creator had enjoyed pressing a thumb into it, a perfect little indent that drew her curious gaze.

His lips were broad and his jaw covered in stubble. His nose was long, straight and autocratic, but it was his eyes that robbed her lungs, momentarily, of the ability to pump air out of her body. They were eyes shaped like almonds, a dark grey in colour, rimmed in thick black lashes that curled in a way Amelia was both dumbfounded by and jealous of. They were eyes that seemed to tell stories, flickering with emotions and thoughts she couldn't decode.

'Well?' he asked again, gruff, but a smile on his lips softened the word. 'May I enter?'

'Yeah.' The word was breathy. She cleared her throat. 'Of course.'

He shrugged out of his jacket, revealing a shirt that had suffered several drops of rainwater. It was a simple gesture—showing the breadth of his chest and the sculptured perfection of his torso.

She swept her eyes shut for a moment and then collected herself, offering an apologetic grimace before moving in a little. 'I'm sorry; I don't get many visitors.'

'Apparently,' he drawled. And then his smile deepened to reveal even white teeth. Her stomach flipped in on itself. 'And so a meat cleaver is how you choose to defend yourself?'

She found herself nodding with mock gravity. 'I feel it's only fair to warn you: I have a black belt in kitchen instruments.'

'Do you?'

'Oh, you should see me wield a potato peeler.'

His laugh was a low rumble from deep in his belly and his eyes were assessing. She wanted to look away but found her gaze held by his, as though trapped. 'Another time,' he said.

'You can unarm yourself,' he added. 'I assure you I don't mean you any harm.'

'I'm sure you don't but I feel I have to point out that very few murderers announce their intentions, do they?'

'I suppose not.'

'So it's quite possible you're just planning the best way to kill me without making a fuss.'

'Except that I've already explained why I'm here,' he responded with a grin that seemed to breathe butterflies into her belly. He looked around her cottage with lazy curiosity.

Amelia didn't have guests often—a few of the teachers from school had come around for her birthday earlier in the year, and once she'd had a student after school, as a favour for the parents, but generally Amelia kept to herself.

What was the point of country solitude if you chose to surrender it?

She tried to see the house as an outsider might—the quaint decorations, the homely simplicity of her furnishings, the absence of any photographs, the abundance of paperback novels and fresh flowers.

'Ah, yes, your proposition,' she murmured. 'Please—' She gestured towards the lounge.

He moved ahead of her and she realised she was staring at his rear, distracted by the way his trousers framed his tight, muscular bottom. Distracted by the way just looking at him was making her nerves buzz into overdrive.

She had practically no experience with men, besides a few casual lunch dates with Rick Steed, the deputy headmaster. And those had ended with chaste kisses to the cheek, nothing particularly distracting or tempting.

As a teenager, she'd railed against the life she'd been sucked into, hating the expectation that because her mother had been renowned both for her beauty and sexually free attitude Amelia must be exactly the same.

She'd begun to suspect she was, in fact, frigid. Completely devoid of any normal sexual impulse or desire. That had suited her fine. What did she need a man for when she had all the men the books in her life afforded?

What indeed? she thought to herself as he turned to face her.

'Nice place.'

'Thank you.'

He was quiet, watching her, and ingrained manners and a need to fill the silence had her offering, 'Can I get you a drink?'

'Thank you.' He nodded.

'What would you like? Tea? Coffee?'

He arched a brow. 'At this hour?'

Heat suffused her cheeks at her own naivety. 'Wine?'

'Wine would be fine.'

'Have a seat. I won't be a minute.'

CHAPTER TWO

HER LOUNGE WAS even cosier—if that was possible—than the exterior of this country cottage had promised.

Delicate and pretty, and oh, so feminine, with soft cushions and blankets everywhere and pictures of flowers on the walls. It was cosy, homely and warm, but his mind was only half-focused on his surroundings. He was mulling over the proposition he'd come here to offer—and what he'd do if she refused.

Already he could see that Amelia diSalvo was different to what he'd expected.

Did that matter? Did it fundamentally change what he needed from her? And what she'd agree to?

His research showed that she'd been inactive in the business, not attending meetings of any kind. She was on the board but didn't contribute; it was clear she had no interest in the day-to-day operations of diSalvo Industries.

But would she be easily convinced to sell her shares to him?

Would she recognise his name and recall the bitter rivalry that had engulfed their families? Would she then have to launch straight into his backup plan? The idea of revealing his machinations to this woman hadn't bothered him an hour earlier but, standing in her living room, suddenly he wasn't in a rush to reveal his reasons for coming to Bumblebee Cottage late in the evening.

Which was absurd given that he'd had an investigator searching for her for over a year. Absurd given that he'd jumped on a flight as soon as she'd been located, with scant regard for the timing of things. If he'd been patient, he could have spent the night in London and driven into the countryside first thing the following morning, catching her in the daytime rather than on a rainy summer evening.

But he was here, and he wouldn't let himself get distracted by the fact that she wasn't the hard and cynical heiress he'd imagined. Nor by the fact she seemed kind of sweet and funny, and lived in a house that was like a tribute to quaint history.

He had spent his adult life setting things right, avenging this feud, and now he was within striking distance. All that stood between himself and success was this one tiny woman.

She was different to what he'd expected, but she was still a diSalvo and she still held the key to his ultimate revenge.

He had to remember that.

It was impossible to say why she felt as if she needed a moment to steady herself in the kitchen, but Amelia took several, sucking in a deep breath and then another and another as she reached for a bottle of wine and a corkscrew. All the wines she'd been given as gifts had actual corks.

She lifted it out easily enough and poured a measure into two glasses—her plans for a cup of tea falling by the wayside as she thought it would give her some fortifying courage.

Wine glasses in hand, she moved back into the lounge. And froze.

He was simply standing, staring at one of the pictures of hydrangeas she'd painted in watercolours, and it was that image of him that did something completely unexpected to her insides.

He was so utterly masculine in the midst of her living space and yet there was something strangely perfect about seeing him there. She stared at him, at the harshness of his face in profile, the strength of his body, broad shoulders and a narrow waist, legs that looked strong and athletic, and her pulse began to speed and her heart was trembling.

Oh, God, what was happening to her? Her mouth was dry and when she lifted her reluctant gaze back to his face she saw he'd turned and a hint of sardonic amusement danced in the depths of his eyes, bringing another flush of pink to her cheeks.

'Here,' she muttered, pushing the wine glass towards him.

He held her gaze as he took it, a smile playing about his lips. '*Gracias.*'

'You're Spanish?' she heard herself say and then winced. Why was she making small talk with him?

'*Sí.*' The word resonated with something spicy and mysterious and, despite the fact it was now raining, she was reminded of the day's sunshine and warmth.

She needed to focus. Why was he here?

'What's your name?'

'Antonio Herrera,' he said, and Amelia frowned, her eyes sweeping shut for a moment.

She felt his gaze, heavy and intent on her face, and her skin goosebumped once more. There was something in her mind, a memory, but it was distant and when she tried to grab it, to focus on it, the thing slipped away from her, like trying to catch a piece of soap that had been dropped into the bath.

'I know that name.'

'Do you?' he murmured, the words throaty.

He held his wine glass to hers, a salute, and she completed it on autopilot. Only their fingertips brushed together and it was as though Amelia had been thrown from an aeroplane. Her stomach twisted in a billion knots and she was in freefall, everything shifting and pulling and nothing making sense. The world was over-bright and her senses jangling. His eyes were merciless, pinning her to the spot, and from grey to black they went once more. She couldn't speak, couldn't move.

'Why do I know your name?' she asked when the answer hadn't come to her. Then, like a bolt of lightning, she remembered. 'Oh! Of course!'

Did his shoulders tighten? Or was she imagining it? 'Yes?'

Hadn't she realised he was a man used to being in command? A figure of dominance and assertiveness?

'You're that guy,' she said, clicking her fingers together. 'I read about you a while ago. You bought that airline and saved all those people from getting fired.'

'Being made redundant,' he clarified. 'And that's not why I bought the airline.'

'No?'

'It was going for a song.' He shrugged.

'I see,' she said thoughtfully, wondering why he was downplaying the altruism of the purchase. He didn't really care about twenty thousand people poised to be out of work if the airline went bust? Or did he want her to think he didn't care?

Her eyes narrowed speculatively. 'And you invest in schools in eastern Europe. And hospitals.'

He arched a brow. 'You seem to know quite a bit about me.'

'It was a long opinion piece,' she explained, her cheeks heating. 'And I like to read the paper. From cover to cover.' She was babbling a little. When she'd moved to her father's home, she'd been surrounded by men like this. Well, not *precisely* like this; he was somewhat unique. But men who were just a little too much of everything. Too handsome, too sharp, too rich.

And she'd never felt overawed by those qualities before.

Having seen her mother fall under their spell time and time again, she'd always been determined to remain immune to those charms.

Then again, she supposed it was a little like the aquarium effect.

'The aquarium effect?' he prompted, and Amelia was mortified to realise she'd been speaking out loud.

She turned away from him, walking unsteadily towards an armchair and sitting in it, then immediately wishing she hadn't when their height disadvantage became even more apparent.

'Please, take a seat.' She gestured towards the sofa.

'Sure. If you'll elaborate,' he drawled. 'I should like to see if you are comparing me to a shark or a seal.'

Her laugh was spontaneous. She watched covertly as he sat—not on the sofa but in the armchair across from hers, his long legs stretched out and dangerously close to her own legs.

'I didn't mean that,' she promised, sipping her wine. 'It's only that when you go to an aquarium you're expecting to see myriad fish, so that even the most beautiful tropical fish or the fluffiest penguin fail to have much of an impact. But if I were walking along the Thames and a beautiful penguin happened to cross my path I'd be basically breathless.'

'Speechless too, I should think, at finding a penguin in central London.'

She nodded, glad he hadn't taken her metaphor the vital step further. Because he was that spectacular piece of wildlife which, when surrounded by men of his ilk, might have left her cold. But here, like this, in her tiny cottage on the outskirts of a small village, smiling at her as though he found her fascinating and unique, how could Amelia fail to be breathless, speechless and hopelessly attracted?

'Have you lived here long?' he asked and she relaxed further as the conversation moved onto far safer ground.

She looked around the lounge, her heart warming at the comfort and beauty of this little room.

'I moved here straight out of University,' she said with a small nod. 'I thought I'd stay only a year or so, but then the cottage came on the market and, what can I say, it was love at first sight,' she said, looking fondly around the small lounge, with its low ceiling and unevenly rendered walls.

'I can see why,' he drawled cynically and she laughed.

'You sound just like my brother!'

Carlo had been just as scathing about the 'relic'. *'Why don't you buy some land and build something bigger? You're a diSalvo,* cara, *and this place isn't fit for a mangy dog.'*

'In what way?'

'Oh, only in so much as he didn't really like Bumblebee Cottage. He's far more into luxury and glamour.'

'And you're not?' Antonio enquired.

'What do you think?' she asked with a lifted brow and a half-smile, gesturing around the room.

'I think the house is charming,' he supplied, leaning forward a little, and his ankle brushed hers, probably by accident, but the effect was the same as if it had been intentional. She sat up straighter, her eyes finding his, a plea and a question in them. 'And so is the occupant,' he added, and now the charge of electricity that flared between them was unmistakably mutual.

She swallowed past the lump in her throat, her eyes round like saucers. His foot brushed hers and now she knew it wasn't an accident she told herself she should pull away. Remove her legs from his reach. Do something, *anything,* to show him she didn't welcome his presumptuous advances.

But oh, how she welcomed them. How she welcomed *him.*

'Thank you.'

It was hard to think straight in that moment. Her body

was charged, her senses in complete disarray, and she was left wondering at the bizarre circumstances that had brought this billionaire tycoon to her door right at the moment when she'd been at risk of sinking into thoughts of loneliness and the pervasive emptiness that came with being alone.

'Well, Antonio—' his name made husky by her too-dry throat '—perhaps you should tell me why you're here?'

He had come to Bumblebee Cottage expecting to hate her. She was a diSalvo; it was written in the stars that he *would* hate her. Only he didn't.

And not only did he *not* hate her; he was actually enjoying himself. He was finding it hard to keep his mind to himself, to concentrate on business when she was smiling at him and joking with him, and when her huge blue eyes kept dropping to his chest, roaming over his breadth as though she were starving and he the only meal around for miles.

And what would she say when he told her the truth of their relationship? What would she say when he explained what he needed from her?

Would she understand? Or would she tell him to get the hell out? Then he'd have to enact plan B, and her smiles would disappear when she realised how close he'd brought her brother to breaking point. And how much he was enjoying that knowledge.

How long had it been since he'd been with a woman? Months. Many months. His father's illness had been sudden and, between the company and Javier's demise, Antonio had barely had time for the distraction of women.

Did that explain the undercurrent of desire that was swirling around them? Was that the reason he was reluctant to tell her why he'd come?

It was the last thing he'd planned for, but now that he sat

opposite Amelia diSalvo he wanted to shelve business and his drive for revenge. Just for a moment. Just for a night.

A temporary delay, that was all, while he enjoyed her company. What was the harm in that?

'Antonio?' she prompted.

He sipped his wine thoughtfully. 'Our grandfathers were friends,' he said slowly, testing her, interested to see what she knew of the feud.

'Were they?' Her nose wrinkled, and his gut kicked. Damn it, she was distracting.

'A long time ago.'

'And that's why you're here?' she prompted.

'In part.'

Her look was teasing. 'Are we playing a guessing game?'

'We can do,' he murmured. 'Let me guess what you're doing in a village like this,' he murmured.

'You don't like it here?'

'It's a far cry from the life you must have lived in Rome.'

'Why do you say that?'

His eyes glittered and with effort he kept the disdain from his voice. 'You're a diSalvo,' he said with the appearance of calm. 'And this cottage is…not.'

She laughed again, a genuine sound of pleasure. 'True.'

Then her eyes fixed on his and he let the silence surround them, aware it was affecting her as much as it was him.

'I feel like I know you,' she said finally, simply, with a sense of surrender that made his body tighten. 'That's crazy, isn't it?'

Yes. It *was*. Everything about this was. She was a part of something he wanted, with all his being, to destroy, and yet in that moment all he could think about was her soft pillowy lips and how they'd feel beneath his. About the fact she was staring at him with huge eyes and her chest was heaving with the force of her breathing.

'I must be losing my mind,' she said, blinking her eyes as if waking from a dream. And then she sipped her wine before offering him a smile that was part self-deprecating and part the most beautiful thing he'd ever seen. What the hell was he thinking, letting himself be so distracted by her, and the way the air around them seemed to crackle and hum? He'd come here with a purpose—a plan he'd set in motion long ago, and *nothing* was going to derail that.

'My grandfather's name was Enrique Herrera. Has your father ever mentioned him?'

She blinked, her huge blue eyes showing obvious confusion. Outside, the rain was falling heavier now but he was barely conscious of it. 'No.'

That was strange. How could Amelia know nothing of a feud that had dominated both his and Carlo's lives?

'We weren't big on *tête-à-tête*,' she explained with a shrug of her slender shoulders that drew his attention to the fine, soft curve of her neck and the hint of cleavage revealed by her simple shirt. Then her eyes lifted to his and his body tightened, his arousal straining against his trousers.

Antonio had spent his adult life moving the pieces into place to destroy Carlo diSalvo, and this woman was a vital part of that. Only through her would he gain control of the one company he desperately wanted and finally avenge the feud that had destroyed his father. Only through appealing to her and then, if it came to it, blackmailing her, would he achieve his goal.

So why was he finding it impossible to sharpen his focus? Because he'd been celibate for months, he told himself. Because he'd been focused on easing his father's last few months of life, and then mourning him appropriately. And now, on acquiring the company that would set all of this to rights.

'My brother might know more about your grandfather,' she said softly, her lips parted. They were beautiful lips—

works of art. Pink and generous, and quick to smile. 'Have you ever spoken to him about Enrique?'

Twice. But conversations with Carlo never ended well. Their hatred was mutual. 'It doesn't matter.' He frowned.

'It must,' she countered, leaning forward a little, and beneath the small coffee table her legs brushed his and his body throbbed with all the awareness that was taking over his mind and soul in that moment. 'For you to have flown all the way here to ask me about him. Or was there something else you wanted to talk to me about?'

Madre de Dios. Antonio had built his company back from dust, he had single-handedly returned Herrera Incorporated to its position as a global powerhouse, and now this one woman was somehow threatening to bring him to his knees?

He stood abruptly and felt her gaze slide up his body. Hungrily. Needily. With the same kind of sensual curiosity that was powering the blood in his own veins.

He'd come to this quaint cottage in the middle of the countryside with one purpose in mind, but now that goal was at war with his body's more immediate needs.

Desire rushed through him as he imagined, for a moment, what it would be like to possess her. Where he was tall and dark, she was fair, all peaches and cream and soft and gentle. Their contrasts fascinated him. What would it be like to lay claim to her body, to drive her wild with desire?

She was a diSalvo! How could he even be thinking like this?

He heard the rustle of clothes as she stood, and then her hand was on his shoulder, turning him to face her. 'Antonio? Is something the matter?'

Everything was the matter! He was so close to bringing her family down, to destroying them as they'd sought to destroy his father, and this one woman was threatening his resolve.

'What is it?' she asked solicitously, her eyes running over his face.

Beautiful eyes in a face that was truly captivating, with long blonde hair he wanted to run his fingers through. He swallowed and then, finally, surrendered to this madness. She was so close, so enticing, and his body was screaming at him to act on his impulses—screw the consequences.

There would be time for revenge later. Afterwards.

With a fatalistic grimace, he lifted a hand and caught her cheek, holding her face steady beneath his. She gasped, her lips parting, a gentle sound of surrender.

And he took her surrender, and he surrendered along-side her.

Slowly, his voice husky, in his native Spanish tongue he murmured, 'You are the most beautiful woman I've ever seen.'

CHAPTER THREE

His words were heavy in the air, mesmerising, and she could only stare at him, and his beautiful body. She could only stare at him, lost to this and him and whatever was happening.

'I…' She frowned, unable to form anything more intelligible. And then her hand was lifting slowly, almost as though it were dragging upwards, pulled by the sheer magnetic force of his body.

She pressed her fingers to his chest, swallowing at the instant bolt of recognition that juddered through her system. Her eyes jerked to his, uncertainty laced with desire, and her fingertips moved across his chest then up to his shoulder.

He made a throaty, groaning sound and then his head dropped forward, or perhaps she pushed up onto the tips of her toes. Whatever it was, on autopilot their lips were meshing, bodies fused together, his broad and hard, his strength emanating from him. His lips moved over hers and she made a gasp of surrender, opening her mouth so that he could deepen the kiss. His hand lifted to the back of her head, his fingers curving around her, holding her where she was so that he could explore her until she was incandescent with pleasure.

'Antonio…' She kissed his name into his mouth, deep into his soul, and felt him answer. Her world was being blasted apart by a simple kiss.

No, there was nothing simple about this—it was crazy

and mad and she knew nothing about him, only his name and that their grandfathers had once been friends. And yet she was his for a song in that moment.

She didn't care what had brought him to her door; she cared only that he was there, and that he wanted her as she did him. Desire—something she had never known nor understood, was rampant in her system now.

As if the heavens were ratifying her surrender to something as elemental as passion, a loud clap of thunder rumbled around the small cottage and a moment later a blade of lightning sliced the sky apart and the house was plunged into darkness. Not complete darkness— Amelia had strung fairy lights generously throughout and, powered by batteries, they offered a golden glow, faint but enough to see by.

He didn't react to the power outage. But his hands roamed her body, running over her sides, finding the hem of her shirt and pushing it, so achingly slowly, up her body so that her skin was covered in goosebumps, her nipples tight against the simple cotton of her bra. He broke the kiss, pulling away from her just long enough to rip her shirt over her head and she pushed her arms skywards at the same time, as fevered as he. In that brief moment of separation their eyes met and something passed between them—an understanding, a commitment to this, come what may— and then he was kissing her again, this time dragging his mouth from her lips to her throat, flicking her with his tongue so that she whimpered with the strength of sensations he was stirring.

He pushed at his own shirt as his mouth claimed hers, dispensing with the fabric confines so his chest was bare.

Her fingers ran over his body without meaning or intent, certainly without forethought, and then her hands found his trousers and, of their own accord, her fingers were loosening his belt buckle then moving to the button and zip, push-

ing at them while his kiss held her body utterly captive. He
stood out of his trousers as she pushed at them, and then
her hands were curving around his naked buttocks, feeling his warmth in a way that was elemental and ancient.

He made a growling noise of awareness and dropped
his hands to her back, pulling her hard against him so she
could feel the strength of his arousal for herself. Surprise
made her eyes flare wide and she swallowed, but then he
was kissing her again, and now he lifted her as though
she weighed nothing and she wrapped her legs around his
waist and he rolled his hips so that his erection found her
feminine heart, the pressure through the fabric of her jeans
enough to make her cry out at what was to come.

He whispered words in Spanish and then he eased her
to the ground, just for a moment, so he could retrieve his
wallet from his trousers. He pulled out a condom. No, con-
doms, she corrected with pink cheeks, and she opened her
mouth, knowing she needed to say something, to tell him
that she was a virgin, because she was sure he wouldn't
enjoy discovering that fact for himself. But then his hands
came to her jeans and he was unfastening them, pushing
them down her legs, and he crouched in front of her and
brought his mouth to her inner thigh and she was lost again.
She tangled her fingers in his hair, throwing her head back
as he kissed her legs.

And then he dragged her simple cotton briefs down her
body and she was complicit, stepping out of them. In the
back of her mind, in the small part of her brain that was
still capable of rational thought, she was surprised by how
unselfconscious she was. She was almost naked in front of
him and she didn't care.

He brought his mouth to the apex of her thighs and
flicked his tongue against her womanhood and now Amelia cried out louder, harder, as pleasure licked through her
like wild flames. She said his name over and over again,

and her fingers ran faster through his hair before dropping to his shoulders and holding on tight. Pleasure was a rollercoaster and she was buckled in, riding it harder and faster, unable to stop the rush of momentum—not wanting to either.

His mouth drove her over the edge and she cried out as an explosion of delight, unlike anything she'd ever imagined, much less known, blew away the last vestiges of any idea that she might not be a sexual being. If this was sex, she could easily become an addict.

But there was no time to recover. He was straightening, lifting himself up, and in one movement he snaked a hand behind her back and unclasped her bra, and she pushed out of it at the same time. His head came crashing down to her breasts, his lips moving from one nipple to the next, circling her sensitive flesh, and desire was rampant in her bloodstream, running like a pack of leopards through her system.

She heard the opening of the condom and felt his hands move against her stomach and something, some thought, was pushing at her brain, but she couldn't catch it. Pleasure was her all—nothing mattered beyond the feelings he was invoking. She was a wildling, abandoned completely to this, and only this.

His hands on her hips were strong and commanding; he lifted her easily and, in her tiny kitchen, he pressed her against the wall and she cried his name, 'Please, please, please,' begging him for a release she couldn't articulate beyond knowing that it was a necessity.

His eyes, glowing in the soft light, burned into hers for several beats. 'You want this.' It was a statement but it dragged her out of the drugging haze of desire, if only for a second. He needed an answer.

An answer beyond her constant begging?

'Yes,' she groaned. 'Oh, God, yes, please, Antonio. I need this.'

And his dark eyes sparked with something new, something like relief and determination, and he moved his body forward and brought her down on his length in one swift, possessive movement.

She froze as the invisible barrier of her innocence was taken by him, and stiffened as an unwelcome and sharp pain pushed all pleasure aside.

He swore in Spanish, sensing what had happened, and she winced, and then his eyes held hers and he whispered softer words, Spanish words, and he wrapped his arms around her, pulling her from the wall, holding her tight, keeping himself inside her and holding her close to him as the pain subsided.

Pleasure returned and it was different and more demanding than before, because he was inside her and muscles she hadn't known she possessed were being stretched and taunted and desire was being stirred that demanded an answer.

'Please,' she said again and he lifted a hand to her cheek, curving it in his palm.

'You are sure, *querida*?'

'Yes.' She nodded.

And, with a look she couldn't interpret, he began to move again, softly this time, gently, and he pressed her against the wall, and he kissed her as his body stirred her back to fever pitch, and he watched her as she blew apart for a second time, this time in his arms and with his erection deep inside her.

And then he eased her back to the ground, her feet on the floor, but only for a second. He scooped down and lifted her, cradling her to his chest as he carried her upstairs, along the hallway. The lighting here was dimmer than downstairs; she had only a few strings of lights on the landing. He looked in one room first—her study—and the next was her bedroom, and apparently there was sufficient light for him to make out at least the shape of the bed. He strode in, laying her down on the mattress gently, then standing. She could just make out the silhouette of his body in the darkness of the house.

Her breath was rushed and she was grateful there was no lighting, glad he wouldn't be able to see the tangle of emotions swirling in her eyes.

'You should have told me,' he said simply, but there was no recrimination in the words, only regret. And then he brought his body over hers and his lips caught hers, and he kissed her as his arousal found its way to her core once more. She wrapped her legs around his waist and he pushed inside her and she groaned as pleasure already began to build anew.

'Your first time should not be with a man you hardly know,' he said, but she barely heard. The words were hoarse and she was way beyond logical, rational thought. When he kissed her his tongue duelled with hers in time with his body's possession of hers and this time, when she found release, he came with her, holding her tight, kissing her, passion saturating them both.

He stayed where he was, inside her, straddling her, but sat straighter; it was impossible to discern anything in his features owing to the blackness of her room.

But his hands found hers and his fingers weaved through hers, holding her, reassuring her.

'I had no idea,' he said.

'I know that.' Now that the bright burst of passion had receded, she had room to feel self-conscious. Not regret, not remorse, only a desire that she'd been better able to meet him on a level of experience closer to his. 'I probably should have told you.'

She was glad it was dark and that he couldn't see her blush and that she couldn't see his face—and the irritation she was sure would be there.

'Yes,' he agreed simply. 'If only so I could have made it perfect for you.'

She lifted her hands to his chest, running her fingers over his muscles thoughtfully. 'That was perfect,' she promised. 'I had no idea…'

His laugh was soft and, inside her, he jerked with the movement and she let out a soft moan as embers of pleasure began to stir anew.

'I mean it,' she repeated huskily. 'I never really got the whole sex thing.'

At that he sobered and when he spoke his voice was husky. 'I'm surprised to hear it.'

He might have meant it as a general throwaway comment, but that was unlikely. He came to her that night knowing who she was, knowing her name, because their grandfathers had been friends. He knew more about her than she did him, and that certainly included knowledge of her mother and her behaviour. 'I think lots of people expect me to be just like her,' she said with a small shrug. 'And I'm not.'

'You didn't want to be,' he clarified gently, and he pulled away from her and rolled them at the same time, so she made a squawking sound of surprise. He held her close to his body, tucked in one arm, and she relaxed against him. His fingers stroked down her back and she sighed softly. New pleasures were vibrating inside her.

'No,' Amelia agreed, hating that it still felt like a betrayal to admit that.

'You haven't dated?'

'Of course I have,' she was compelled to declare, hating what a novice she was! His fingers paused in their stroking for a moment before resuming their leisurely trail along her back. 'But never seriously, never for long.' She shrugged against his side. 'Whereas you, I imagine, have a *long* list of ex-girlfriends.'

'Not really,' he said, surprising her. 'I don't really date.'

Of course. How gauche of her. 'Lovers, then.'

He laughed. 'Enough,' he agreed after a moment.

She bit down on her lip. 'But I bet it's been a long time since you were with a virgin.'

'I've never been with a virgin,' he said simply. 'Not even my first time.'

She blinked at that confession. 'Seriously?'

'Yeah.'

So she was his first? She couldn't explain it, but she liked that. It was as though they'd both shared a new experience together, and it meant more to her than it should.

'How do you feel?' The gravelled question sent her pulse firing anew.

'Relaxed and satisfied,' she purred and he laughed, a throaty sound of wry amusement.

'I'm pleased to hear it. Stay here.' And he pulled away from her, standing and moving out of her room.

'What are you doing?' she called after him, but the words were soft, consumed by a yawn. And, instead of asking again, she collapsed back against the bed, closed her eyes and remembered. Remembered the madness in the kitchen that had brought his lips to hers, or was it the other way around? Remembered the way they'd exploded at that first touch and everything had seemed predestined in some way.

A moment later she had her answer, anyway. The sound of the bath running, then the bathroom cabinets being open and shut. She lay there, a smile on her face, listening, and a little while later he returned.

'Are you asleep?'

She squinted one eye open and then realised he couldn't see her. 'No,' she said, sitting up. 'Are you taking a bath?'

He laughed. 'No. You are.'

He reached for her hand and she wriggled off the bed,

standing on legs that had suddenly turned to jelly. He understood and he lifted her once more, so she joked, 'I could get used to this. Like some kind of Rajah.'

He stepped over the threshold, into the bathroom, and her breath caught in her throat. He must have found every candle in the house and the bathroom was glowing and warm, like something out of a fairy tale.

Don't! she alerted her subconscious.

Don't even think like that.

Fairy tales. Don't. Exist.

How many times had she seen her mother go down the rabbit hole of thinking a man was her Prince Charming and that their 'happily ever after' was at the end of the next party or vacation or new home or fresh start? Only to wake up alone, miserable, depressed and looking for consolation in the bottle or vial of whatever drug she was into at the time.

Amelia was not Penny—and that meant knowing, beyond a shadow of a doubt, that fairy tales didn't exist.

Still, fairy tale or not, the bathroom was beautiful in this lighting. The tub was half-filled and an extravagant layer of bubbles sat on top of the water's surface. There was an aroma of lavender in the air—so he'd found her bath oils.

He placed her over the edge of the tub, easing her feet into the water, and she smiled as the perfect warmth wrapped around her legs. She sank into it slowly, lying back against the edge and letting the water enfold her.

'Heaven,' she said softly and then blinked her eyes open to find him staring at her.

'Enjoy it.' His eyes sparked with something like promise and her heart turned over in her chest. 'I'll be waiting.' He retrieved a towel and placed it within easy reach of the bath, then moved to the door. 'Don't fall asleep,' he warned as he left and she smiled.

Fat chance.

She wasn't going to fall asleep all night. Not when she had Antonio Herrera as her own personal pleasure centre. Having discovered what her body was capable of feeling, she wanted more. She wanted everything.

And she wanted him to show her.

He collected his scattered clothes from the kitchen floor, and he dressed with true regret. He didn't want to put barriers up to more pleasure. He wanted to take her to bed and make love to her slowly, to seduce her all night long, like he would any other lover.

But there was danger in that—danger in forgetting why he'd come to her, why he'd spent a year trying to locate her. Why he needed her signature on the documents he'd brought with him, her agreement to sell her shares to him.

He had buried his father a month earlier and there was no way he was going to let his desire for a woman cloud his judgement.

He was so close to achieving his goal, and Amelia diSalvo was the key to that.

Sex with her had been a mistake. A stupid, careless mistake—because it had the power to confuse things between them. Because it muddied the water of what he needed from her.

With a grim expression on his face, he let himself quietly out of the house, walking towards his car with a growing sense of determination. The rain had stopped but the clouds were still overhead, covering the moon and the stars so everything was in pitch darkness.

The documents were on the front seat. He grabbed them out, tucking them under his arm before making his way back to the house. Silence came from upstairs.

He fought a desire to go and check on her, to see if she needed anything. A passionate encounter didn't a relation-

ship make—there was no need for him to play the part of
the solicitous boyfriend. It was better for both of them if he
focused on his reason for being in the cottage.

Revenge was close—so close he could feel it. And it
would be better than anything he'd ever known—even the
pleasure he'd just felt in the bed of his arch-enemy.

CHAPTER FOUR

'I THOUGHT I heard the door.'

She appeared in the lounge and at that moment the lights flickered to life—a stutter at first and then a burst, and her expression showed bemusement.

'You're dressed?' She lifted a brow, padding across the room in only a silk robe. A robe that left little to the imagination, not that he needed to use it. He could remember every single curve and delineation of her body, every indent and hollow. Though he regretted now not making love to her in the brightness of this light, so that he could see her peaches and cream complexion all over, marvel at the contrast of her nipples to her skin.

Damn it—he tightened against his trousers, unwanted desire flooding his system once more.

'What's the matter? You're suddenly struck mute?' Something like uncertainty fluttered in her expression but she covered it quickly. 'I mean, I know that was good, but surely not enough to rob you of the ability to speak.'

His smile was tight on his face. Her easy nature was at odds with the direction of his thoughts.

'I came here tonight to talk to you about something important.'

Confusion clouded her expression. 'Oh. Right. I'd…forgotten. Something to do with our grandfathers?' She blinked, her expression still one of trust, and stepped across the room. 'Surely it can wait?' she implored, lifting a hand to his chest, her eyes meeting his in both a challenge and an invitation.

God, he wished it could wait. But being caught up in the moment, letting passion override common sense once was one thing. It would be quite another to keep exploiting her sensual need, an appetite he had awakened without realising her innocence.

'Not really.' He grimaced. 'Why don't you sit down?'

'I'm fine.' She shook her head as wariness crept into her expression. A wariness he couldn't help but resent.

He nodded, a stiff movement, and lifted his hand to rub his neck. He hadn't thought about what he would say. When he had come to Bumblebee Cottage, he'd expected this to be much like a standard business meeting.

She had something he needed, and he had something he could offer in exchange. Money, in the first instance and, failing that, a promise to bide his time with her brother's business, not to bring him to his knees in a cataclysmic fashion. Blackmail, yes.

Would he still stoop to that, given what they'd just shared?

He straightened his shoulders, his expression tense. Sex was beside the point. It didn't change the facts—he wanted what she had and he'd go to any lengths to acquire it.

Too much rested on his success here, and the hatred he felt for the diSalvo family went deeper than anything he'd shared with Amelia this evening.

'I need you to sign this.' He pulled the contract from his document wallet and placed it on the table—the coffee table they'd sat at only a couple of hours earlier, tension zipping through the room.

Well, there was tension again now, but a different kind altogether.

Her eyes showed confusion and then they skipped away from his. She crossed to the table, close enough that he could breathe in her sweet smell of lavender and vanilla, so close that he could simply reach out and pull her close, forgetting about the damned shares for a moment longer.

She pressed a finger to the contract, drawing it down the title page as she read, then silently flipped it over. She read that and then the next, and finally lifted her eyes back to his face. 'You want to buy my shares in Prim'Aqua? Why?'

'Because without your shares I can't assume a majority ownership.'

She blinked, his clear sentence apparently not making any sense to her. 'It's one of my family's business interests. Why would you want to assume a majority ownership?'

It was like waving a red rag in front of a charging bull.

'Because it was my family's company also,' he said with deceptive calm. 'And I will not rest until it is back in my hands.'

The words hung in the air like little daggers, but they made absolutely no sense. None of this made any sense.

He'd come to her house and, true, she hadn't exactly interrogated him about what he'd wanted but…how could she have known anything like this had brought him to her?

'I presumed you just wanted to talk about our grandfathers!' she said with a shake of her head. 'This can't be real.'

His eyes narrowed and a burst of adrenalin fired in her gut as she recognised in this man a latent power and determination that had been absent for the rest of the evening. He'd been charming and humorous and now she could see that there was a whole other side to him.

'I have acquired thirty-five per cent of the company,' he said, the words soft yet laced with iron-hard determination. 'Your father and brother will never part with their stake, but that does not matter. Not when your shares will give me the majority. I want them.'

'Why?' She pressed her hands to her hips, turning away

from the contract, then immediately wished she hadn't. Because he was wearing a suit and she was dressed in a silk robe and her body hadn't quite caught up with the fact that he was there for business. That she'd slept with a man, given her virginity to a man, who only wanted her shares in a family company. God knew *she* didn't want them—how often had she wished that her father hadn't gifted such a valuable portfolio on her eighteenth birthday? She'd always felt he was making up for lost time, trying to show her with money how valued and loved she was—but money was the last thing she ever wanted.

The assets she had made her feel even more vulnerable and exposed in that superficial world. With her mother's looks and a fortune at her fingertips—it had been a fast track to attracting all the wrong people.

It still was, apparently.

'Our grandfathers were best friends from the time they were boys.' He spoke slowly, as though she didn't have a tight grasp on English. That exasperated her further.

'I don't need to know the history,' she snapped. 'I need to know why these shares matter so much to you that you were willing to come to my home and…and…seduce me, just to get your hands on them.'

At that, he had the decency to look surprised. 'One thing had nothing to do with the other,' he said slowly and reached a hand out for her, a hand of comfort and reassurance, but she batted it away angrily.

'No.' She took a step back; her hip connected with the table. 'The part of the evening where you get to touch me is absolutely at an end.'

He compressed his lips in exasperation. 'I didn't come here intending to sleep with you. But you were so… It just happened,' he said with a shake of his head. 'I didn't plan it.'

'Oh, yes.' She rolled her eyes, shaking with pent-up rage and deep-down hurt. 'It was just convenient that I happened to fall into bed with you, right before you blindsided me by asking me for something worth millions of pounds.'

'You'll see on the contracts that I'm prepared to pay double their value,' he said silkily.

She put her hands on her hips then wished she hadn't. The gesture drew the robe across her front and his attention dropped to her silk-covered breasts, and nipples that were still tight and heavy with arousal.

'I don't need your money,' she spat. 'You think any amount would induce me to sell the shares to *you*?'

'Our grandfathers had a fight. No, it was more than that. It was war,' he said, returning to the original point. 'They'd started Prim'Aqua by joining together two shipping companies they'd inherited from their fathers, and it became the most powerful water-based logistics and transportation company in the world. Both of our families owe their prosperity to Prim'Aqua.'

'Fine, if you say so,' she snapped, moving towards the door. 'But it's *my* father's company now.'

'Your grandfather fooled my grandfather into signing it over—my grandfather trusted him implicitly and signed the deeds without reading.'

'More fool him,' she muttered.

His expression tightened. 'It was a mistake on his part to trust a diSalvo—and that is a lesson I will never forget.' His eyes glittered black when they met hers. 'But I can rectify this, if you will only be reasonable.'

'You dare ask *me* to be reasonable when you've just insulted my whole family? And me?'

'You come from a family of thieves and bastards, Amelia.'

She stared at him; it felt as if he'd morphed into some kind of alien. It took her several seconds to be able to find her tongue and push it into service.

'My God, get the hell out of this house,' she demanded, the words only slightly shaky. 'How dare you think I would give you *anything*? How can you speak of my family with such obvious disgust when you've literally come straight from my bed?'

'Sleeping with you has nothing to do with why I'm here. I did not plan for that to happen, and it is not going to derail me from my course.' His eyes narrowed warningly. 'Nothing will, Amelia.'

The light in the house was so bright, and she could see him clearly now. His ruthless determination was a physical force in the room, a dark shape she would never be able to grapple with.

Her skin paled, her heart lurched. 'You're a real piece of work, aren't you?'

He angled his head away from her and in profile his face was powerful, as if carved from stone, and a muscle jerked in his jaw, throbbing hard as he reined in his temper.

'You have no interest in the shares I want.'

'How do you know that?' she demanded, crossing her arms over her chest.

He turned to face her, his eyes pinning her to the wall. Oh, God, just like the wall he'd held her against when he'd thrust inside her. Her heart gave a strange little double-beat as memories threatened to swallow her whole.

'Since you inherited your stock portfolio, you have attended precisely zero board or shareholder meetings. You do not appear at corporate events...you do not have a bio on the website. You are absent in every way.'

'So?' She rolled her eyes. 'Ever heard of a silent partner?'

'It is not the same thing. You have holed yourself up here, as far as you can get from the seat of power in diSalvo Industries. You do not want to use your shares to control the company—'

'And is that any wonder? When getting involved in my family's business would mean running up against vultures like you?'

His nostrils flared as he expelled a rapid breath. 'You think I am a *vulture* for wanting to take back what was stolen from me? Prim'Aqua is my birthright…'

'As much as it is mine and Carlo's,' she interrupted firmly, her cheeks flushing pink. 'You have as large a stake in the company as I do. And larger than my brother's too. So what's your problem?'

'I do not want your family having *any* part of it,' he said with icy simplicity. 'Your grandfather stole it and I intend to take it back.' He softened his voice slightly. 'Only I am *not* stealing it. This is a business transaction, plain and simple. You have something I want and I'm prepared to pay you for it.'

'You're unbelievable. Do you realise that if you'd told me this when you first arrived I *might* have heard you out? But how can you think, after what just happened between us, you can lay all this at my feet and I won't be angry?'

'Because you're a sensible, mature woman,' he said. 'And I believe you capable of seeing that business is separate to the personal.'

'There is no business here!' she roared. 'We just had sex! Not even an hour ago! You took my virginity and it was… just a way to soften me up towards you, so that I'd agree to anything you wanted.'

He swore in Spanish and shook his head. His face was deathly serious, his face harsh with intent. When he spoke, the words were slow and grated from him, indignation heavy in each accented syllable. 'If you think I would ever stoop to something so low, then you have no idea who you're dealing with.'

'No, clearly I don't,' she agreed scathingly. 'Now, please go.'

'You do not want me to leave without those contracts,' he said, the words softly menacing.

It took a moment for the penny to drop, to make sense of the words he'd just issued. 'Are you threatening me?'

Something like sympathy crossed his face. 'No. I am threatening your brother.'

Now Amelia was frozen still, her breath coming in fits and spurts, her eyes holding his as she tried to make sense of what he meant.

'Carlo foolishly picked up our families' rivalry some years ago.' Antonio spoke calmly, emotions carefully blanked from his voice. 'In truth, I'm surprised he never spoke to you of it.'

'He knew I had no interest in that side of things.' She wrapped her arms around her chest.

Antonio's expression tightened. 'He wanted to ruin my father once and for all, to destroy my family's legacy as the final step in this feud. By the time I took over the company it was a shambles; my father was destroyed, his life's work ruined.' His eyes glinted with the harsh recollection, and there was something else there too. A grief that threatened to shake her sympathetic heart to the core. 'It has taken me a long time to rebuild Herrera Incorporated, but I have done it, *querida*, and then some.'

And then some.

The words sat between them and a *frisson* of tension ran down her spine because there was a threat in that word, surely. A threat and a promise.

'What does that mean?'

He seemed to be waging a war within himself, as though there was a part of him that wanted to spit the salient facts at her feet and a part of him that wanted to protect what they'd just shared. The former won, apparently.

'I have invested wisely these last few years, steadily amassing shares in diSalvo business interests so that I now find I own more than half of your brother's various companies.'

She sucked in a breath. Surely it was a lie, an exaggeration?

'I don't believe you,' she said after a beat had passed, her mind working fast to keep up. 'Carlo would *never* have allowed that to happen.'

'It is easy to acquire anything if you are prepared to bide your time.'

Her stomach twisted into dozens of knots. 'To what end, though?' The depth of his hatred made no sense to Amelia. 'Surely you don't *want* diSalvo investments?'

'Want them? No.' He lowered his voice. 'I want to destroy them. I want to take your brother's legacy and crush it into the ground, as he did my father's. Only I will destroy him beyond any hope of redemption. I will only rest when he is destitute and starving, so that the memory of having a wallet full of money is all he has to warm him in his old age.'

She stared at this passionate man who had only a short time earlier taught her body what it was capable of feeling, the pleasures he'd lavished her with! And now she saw the beast of hatred that moved within him and shivered, for there was such coldness there, such determination, that she didn't doubt him capable of carrying out what he'd threatened.

'You honestly think that's going to fix what happened to your father?'

He stayed quiet for a moment and then shrugged his broad, powerful shoulders. Her traitorous body gave a little jerk of awareness and she wanted to slap herself for feeling *anything* for this man except disgust. 'Carlo played with fire. I am simply making him feel the heat of those flames.'

She gaped. 'That's preposterous!'

But he was, apparently, beyond arguing. He spoke with a calm insistence. 'There are two options here, *querida*.

Sell me your shares in Prim'Aqua and it is over. Done. I will release the grip I have on his empire and he will be safe. Or, if you keep your shares and deny me ownership of a company that is rightfully mine, I will destroy the rest of your family's businesses. I have the power to tank them, and I will do it. And, what's more, I will damned well enjoy it.'

Her heart was thumping. 'You'll destroy a huge proportion of your wealth if you do that.'

'I have more than enough money,' he said carelessly.

'You're unbelievable.'

'Believe it.' His eyes locked onto hers and she shivered with the force of his power. 'And make a decision.'

'A decision? My decision is for you to get out of my house!' She wrenched the door open. 'Or I'll call the police!'

He stared at her for several moments, towering over her, and his breathing matched her own, then he shook his head. 'I do not want to fight with you.'

'I don't want to fight with you either,' she said and she shoved at his chest. 'Get out of my house! Right now!'

She didn't think he was going to go. And she hated that there was a very small part of her that didn't want him to go, that wanted him to stay and fight and plead with her. To apologise for what he'd done, or tried to do. To take it all back and say he didn't hate her family, that he wasn't actively working to bring down her brother and father's commercial interests.

But that was a very, very small part. Most of Amelia diSalvo hated Antonio Ferrara with every single bone in her body in that moment and couldn't wait to see the back of him.

'This isn't over,' he said, but it was soft, almost apologetic, and then he stalked out of the door and, she hoped, out of her life.

* * *

Antonio wasn't surprised to receive a call from Carlo diSalvo the next day, but he was surprised at the effect the call had on him.

He could not speak to Carlo without thinking of Amelia, and the way her body had responded to his. He couldn't close his eyes without seeing her tiny cottage and the fairy lights she'd decorated almost every surface with—and there was something so *her* about that design choice.

'You're a bastard,' Carlo snapped down the phone line. 'Did you really think I wouldn't find out?'

Antonio stared at the view of London he had from his penthouse, Mayfair sprawling with all its Georgian beauty before him, opening up to a verdant Hyde Park. 'I didn't much care,' Antonio said, not completely honest. Because he *did* care about something.

Amelia.

It was ridiculous, but he hadn't been able to get her out of his head since leaving Bumblebee Cottage the night before. Nor could he shake the feeling that, for the first time in his life, he might not have handled things in the best possible way. He hadn't achieved his aim, and he'd made things monumentally more difficult by sleeping with the enemy.

'So what's your plan?' Carlo demanded, switching to his native Italian.

Antonio followed him effortlessly. 'To destroy you. No, to do more than destroy you. I will eviscerate you. I will take everything you care about and destroy it, just for the satisfaction of seeing you suffer. My life has become a testament to your ruination.'

Carlo cursed down the phone line. 'You actually think you'll be able to succeed in that?'

'It is already done,' Antonio said, a wolfish smile spreading across his features. He disconnected the call and pushed all thoughts of Amelia from his mind. Sleeping with her hadn't been part of the plan, but that didn't matter. It was beside the point, just like he'd said to her. Sex had nothing to do with business, and this business was something he'd spent long years planning for.

He scrolled to his personal lawyer's number and held the phone to his ear.

'Herrera,' he spoke without preamble when the call connected. 'I need to see you. It's about the diSalvo situation.' He reclined in his chair, staring straight ahead and seeing only the gleam of success. The satisfaction of long-awaited revenge.

And the pair of big blue eyes that haunted him as he told his lawyer to begin tanking diSalvo interests?

They were just eyes—he would forget them soon enough. He would forget her too. Because nothing mattered more than righting the wrongs of the past. Nothing, and no one. For his father, he would succeed.

CHAPTER FIVE

AMELIA STARED AT the name across the foyer, emblazoned in solid gold letters: Herrera Inc. Her tummy was in knots as she waited in the echoing silence.

Not knots of anxiety, she hastened to remind herself. Knots of anger. Fury. Panic. Disbelief that six weeks after spending the night with a wolf in sheep's clothing—or no clothing, as the case had been—it had been necessary to fly to Spain and wait in his office on a day that was hot and sticky, when she would have far preferred to be home in her lovely little cottage with only her books and an enormous pot of tea for company.

She'd thought about calling him and breaking the news to him over the phone. It would have been satisfying to have the power to deliver the life-changing words and then disconnect the call, letting him stew on the discovery as she had been for almost a week. But this wasn't news one delivered over the phone, and she'd accepted that, even when it meant she would need to see Antonio once more.

Her face was pale and, though she didn't realise it, the immaculate secretary of Antonio Herrera was watching her from beneath hooded eyes.

'He won't be much longer, madam,' the woman assured her.

Did she really look that bad?

She'd mostly escaped the dreaded morning sickness, but of course it had reared its head that morning and she'd been feeling queasy all day.

She'd be better once this part was over. She had a plan, and it was simple.

Antonio, I'm pregnant, but I'm sure you won't want any part of the pregnancy or the baby's life, given that it's the devil's spawn.

Or, *Antonio, I'm pregnant, and you can't offer any amount of money that will induce me to sell this baby to you. Not everything is for sale.*

Then there was the option where she just blurted names at him, every single one she could think of, obscenities and curses, in all the languages she knew.

She ground her teeth together, her hand curled around the strap of her bag, her mouth dry. She thought about getting another cup of water from the dispenser, but she must have already drunk a litre since arriving in his office almost an hour earlier.

If he'd known she was coming, she would have blamed him for keeping her waiting. But she'd intentionally used a fake name to see him, pretending to be a journalist writing an opinion piece for a broadsheet newspaper. Eventually the assistant had cracked, offering a fifteen-minute slot. But apparently Antonio viewed journalists with disdain, if his inability to stick to the schedule was anything to go by.

Another fifteen minutes later and the door cracked open. A man emerged first—not Antonio. Blond, with green eyes and tanned skin, wearing a suit but looking like he'd much prefer to be in board shorts and riding a wave. When he spoke, it was with an American accent. 'Great to see you again, brother.' He grinned, and he was film-star-handsome. Sigh…

Damned hormones. She stood up, knowing Antonio's appearance was imminent and that the last thing she wanted was to be at a height disadvantage from the outset. Strength was imperative, even when it was simply a fraud.

Sure enough, a moment later he was in the doorway,

only he wasn't alone. A young boy was in his arms—only four or five, she guessed, but with the unmistakable facial features of a child born with Down's Syndrome. And the young boy was smiling at Antonio as though he were the second coming.

'You give your mother a high five from me, okay?'

And the little boy, on cue, lifted his hand and whacked it against Antonio's. 'Again!'

Antonio laughed, his eyes crinkling in the corners, and obliged, and Amelia had to dig her fingernails into her palms to stop from reacting.

Hormones! Tears were stinging her eyes suddenly at the sight of this man she *hated,* who happened to be the father of her baby, looking so perfectly at home with children. She blinked the tears away, assuming a look of passive impatience that was at odds with the lurching in her gut. And she felt it, the moment his eyes began to move to hers.

She glared at him, her expression icy.

'Amelia?' He looked genuinely surprised, and she was glad.

His friend followed Antonio's gaze and then reached for the little boy.

'We'll get out of your hair, man. Just don't leave it long before you get out to Venice Beach, yeah?'

Antonio didn't respond. He was staring at Amelia, not speaking, simply looking. Did he think he could intimidate her? That he could make her feel anything at all any more?

She squared her shoulders and straightened her spine, staring at him with all the disdain she felt.

He'd used her.

He'd come to her house and charmed her into bed and she'd fallen in with his plans like the naïve, innocent fool she was, and hadn't she learned her lesson? The reason she'd kept men like this at bay her whole life had unravelled before her.

The blond man and child left, the latter waving enthusiastically at Antonio as he went. But Antonio didn't notice. His gaze was fixed squarely on Amelia.

After several moments, he crossed the foyer, his stride long, and in that time he pulled himself together.

'I didn't realise you were in Madrid,' he said conversationally, as though they communicated regularly and she had simply omitted to mention the detail.

'I came to see you,' she said, glad when he didn't hold a hand out to shake hers, nor attempt to kiss her cheek. There was ice between them now.

'Really?' He arched a brow and she wanted to slap him then, and his smug assumption that she'd come for personal reasons. For sexual reasons.

Her glare, she hoped, would put paid to any such ideas. 'I presume you have an office in which we might speak privately?'

'Of course,' he murmured throatily, putting a hand in the small of her back.

And trumpets flared in her mind, bleating 'hallelujah' at the simple touch and she ground her teeth together in utter rejection of that. 'I'm quite capable of walking, thank you very much,' she said flatly and stepped to the side, away from him.

She only just caught the look of bemusement on his secretary's face before she spun on her heel and stalked towards his office.

So she was still furious with him, obviously. But she was here, in his office, and he had to think it had something to do with Prim'Aqua. No doubt the moves he was making against Carlo were starting to worry her family—and so they should. So had she chosen to come to him, like a lion to the slaughter? To beg him to back off?

It was pretty obvious she hadn't turned up in Madrid

looking for round two of their off-the-charts sexual chemistry. His body jerked with disappointment because, no matter what he told himself about that night, there was a reason it had been tormenting his dreams.

Physically, they made some strange kind of sense.

Their bodies had moved as though they'd been designed for one another, but that meant nothing. Sex was sex. He walked a pace behind her, hating that he was staring at her as though she was a dessert on a buffet, knowing he could hardly stop himself.

Instead of the jeans and casual shirt she'd been wearing that night at Bumblebee Cottage, she'd chosen a pair of sleek black pants and a silk blouse that was a dangerous reminder of the robe she'd pulled on after her bath. She wore heels too, thin and spindly, giving her an extra few inches of height.

She'd dressed up.

For him?

At the door to his office she stepped aside, waiting. He pushed the door open then held it for her, noting with what he wished was amusement that she gave him as wide a berth as the doorway allowed.

His office was everything she'd expected. Just like her father's. And her brother's. And no doubt all the other dictatorial, selfish corporate tycoons who ruled the finance world. Enormous, with huge windows that framed a stunning view, impressive oak desk, state-of-the-art computer screens, a wall-mounted smart TV for conferences, a boardroom table of shiny timber surrounded by leather chairs, and white leather sofas. Different materials perhaps, but the same essence as the offices she'd been in before.

There were some indications of his personal taste. A black and white photograph of the Millau Viaduct, a small pottery *toro* on his desk, a stunning modern sculpture that was gunmetal grey and silver, and utterly striking.

She ignored these details though, and all the ostentatious signs of wealth, placing her handbag on a chair and turning to face him.

And she felt as if she'd been kicked in the gut.

God, he was handsome.

So handsome, with eyes that were laced with enquiry and hair that she ached to run her fingers through.

Stupid, stupid traitorous body.

Pushing any such thoughts from her mind, she tried to summon the words she'd prepared.

'Would you like a drink?'

Her stomach heaved at the very suggestion. 'No.' The word was abrupt, and she winced. 'No, thank you,' she corrected softly.

She paced to the window overlooking Madrid and stared out at the ancient city. In the distance, she could see a slice of Gaudí poking impishly from behind a far more sensible high rise, and she was reminded of a child hiding around the corner, awaiting a scolding. Gaudí's irreverence was one of her favourite things about Spain.

'Well,' he said quietly, and the word ran down her spine like warm honey. 'What can I do for you, Amelia?'

Her name on his lips tripped her heart up a thousand gears and she took a steadying breath, reminding herself that she was in control of her body, not the other way around.

When she hadn't spoken, after a moment, he said, 'I have an appointment any minute.'

'No, you don't.' She swallowed. 'I'm your appointment.'

When she turned to face him, she could see he was analysing this, examining her statement for meaning. 'You pretended to be a journalist, simply to see me again?'

She nodded crisply.

'Why not just give my assistant your name?'

'Because I took a perverse pleasure in surprising you,' she said honestly, and was rewarded with the hint of a smile at the corners of his lips.

It was too familiar—too familiar for what they were to one another, and what they'd shared. Theirs had been no love story; it had been two strangers in a thunderstorm. She'd been caught up in the romance—the storm had raged and he'd arrived, offering refuge from a clawing sense of isolation. She'd been a means to an end for him, her virginity unimportant collateral in his quest to draw her under his spell.

'You have surprised me,' he agreed.

You haven't seen anything yet, she thought to herself with a wry shake of her head.

Was she really going to do this?

Of course! What was the alternative? Have his baby and never tell him? Just like her mother had done to her father?

No way would her baby know the pain of that. Amelia had grown up with no idea who her father was—half the time she wasn't even sure her mother knew. She'd been a secret baby, a shameful love-child, unwanted, an accident, and there was no way her baby would ever grow up feeling like she had.

And didn't Antonio deserve to know? Not just for the sake of their baby, but because this was his baby too?

Amelia might not have liked what had happened with her and Antonio; she certainly didn't like the fact that he'd come to her cottage and seduced her without telling her they were part of an ancient blood feud, then expected her to hand over thirty per cent of a family business to him, but he was still a person. A person with inalienable rights. A man who would soon become a father and of course he deserved to know that.

Heaven help her if he decided he wanted to be a part of the child's life on a regular basis, because that would mean she would also have to see him too, she supposed.

But Amelia doubted he'd want much to do with their child. It would be, after all, a diSalvo.

The thought had her tilting her chin, her eyes sparking defiantly with his. 'This won't take long,' she assured him, thinking gratefully of the return flight she'd booked for later that same day.

'Go on,' he encouraged, perching his bottom on the edge of the desk, stretching his long legs in front of him, crossed at the ankles.

She ignored the throb low in her abdomen, the instant recognition of power and strength, the memory of how those legs had held her to the wall, pinning her with total ease, or straddled her body as he moved inside her. She looked away, her mouth dry. 'Perhaps I will have some water,' she said, stalking across the room to where the drinks were set up. She poured a small glass with hands that weren't quite steady and sipped from it, then shut her eyes as her stomach instantly rejected the offering.

Damn it. She pressed her fingertips to the bench, blinking, willing her insides to calm down, not to be ill. Not here! Not now!

'At the risk of appearing rude, I don't have all day.'

It was exactly what she needed to bring herself back to the moment. She spun around, then wished she hadn't when the room swayed a little. 'You're so far past appearing rude,' she promised firmly. 'And I won't take much of your time.'

His eyes were studying her and she hated that. She hated that he could probably read every emotion that crossed her face, every feeling that was shredding her insides.

'Go on,' he prompted.

'Don't rush me.'

His laugh was sardonic. 'You just told me this won't take long.'

'Yes, well, it doesn't help when you're staring at me as though you'd like to...'

* * *

She didn't finish the sentence but that didn't stop the immediate flash of desire in response to her suggestion. His expression softened as he allowed himself to do exactly what she'd said—to stare at her openly, to run his gaze over her body, remembering it precisely, and then lift to meet her eyes.

'I'm staring at you,' he corrected finally, 'like a man wanting a woman to get to the point.'

That wasn't completely true. Like Scheherazade's King, he was willing her to spin out a story to elongate this encounter.

He was, frankly, still reeling from the fact she was here, in his office. In the weeks after that night, he'd thought about calling her. Hell, he'd contemplated flying back to England, driving to Bumblebee Cottage and demanding she listen to him—ideally in bed.

If she understood the nature of their families' dispute, perhaps she'd look more sympathetically on his offer.

But he'd done neither in the end. Because he couldn't think of seeing her again without seeing her as she'd been that night. The look of betrayal and hurt on her face had made him feel, almost for the first time in his life, ashamed.

And he'd hated that.

So he'd relegated her to the back of his mind, to his 'past', and told himself he'd forget about her.

Because she was a diSalvo, and what point was there in trying to get her to forgive him?

There were more issues between them than a simple one-night stand.

Wrong thought. Wrong thought. His mind threw up the memories and he sank into them, remembering her body, the sounds she'd made as pleasure had caressed her, the way she had kissed him as if her very life depended on it.

'Have you reconsidered?' he prompted, thinking of his more than generous deal to buy her shares in Prim'Aqua—and the way he was deliberately tanking diSalvo interests around the globe. Did she know?

'No—' she narrowed her eyes '—my shares aren't for sale. And I don't think you'll be able to do anything to hurt Carlo either. He's very shrewd, great at what he does. You're no threat to him.'

Antonio almost smiled. She wasn't the first person to underestimate him, but truly she couldn't be more wrong.

'We'll see.' He shrugged with the appearance of calm.

Her eyes narrowed and he had the sense that she was analysing him now, looking for hidden meanings. 'You really hate my family, don't you?'

He expelled a soft breath. 'Is it any wonder?'

Her neck moved delicately as she swallowed, and he realised suddenly that she looked tired. Beneath the make-up she wore—another change since the night in Bumblebee Cottage—he detected the hint of darkening beneath her eyes and a pallor that hadn't been there before.

'So that night, when we slept together, you knew that we could never be more than that one experience?'

The question floored him. But only for a moment—he was Antonio Ferrera and he recovered quickly. 'Do you want it to be more?'

She pulled a face and her answer dripped with sarcasm. 'Yeah, right.'

He smirked to cover his irritation. He didn't like the ease with which she rejected that suggestion. Hell, at that moment he could barely remember that she was a diSalvo, let alone muster enough enthusiasm for their rivalry to care. She was simply Amelia and he was hungry—starving—for her.

'So you are not here to sell me your stake in Prim'Aqua,' he said, straightening, pushing off the desk and taking a stride towards her. 'And you say you are not here to rekindle what we shared that night.' Another stride, bringing him level with her, and the sweetness of her scent almost had him reaching for her and kissing her. How he wanted to relive that experience!

But every line of her body was a warning and a rejection. She was mentally distancing herself from him and he hated that.

'So why have you come?'

Amelia clamped her lips together and dug her fingernails into her palms and she stared at him and reminded herself that he was just a man! There was no need to feel so anxious! Besides, she was absolutely certain he wouldn't want to be a part of her life—or her child's.

'You look pale,' he added with a frown, and inwardly she groaned. She'd done her best to hide the evidence of the past few weeks, but apparently hadn't succeeded.

Some women glowed when they were pregnant and it seemed Amelia wasn't going to be one of them. This very recent bout of nausea combined with a sudden insomnia— no doubt brought on by the realisation she had to tell the father of her baby that she was pregnant—had left her looking drained.

'How I look is hardly relevant,' she murmured.

His frown was infinitesimal. 'Are you sick?'

'Yes, in a sense,' she said, and an urge to laugh, maniacally, overcame her. She ignored it with effort and reached for her water glass once more.

It wasn't that she was afraid of him, but she knew that once she spoke these words aloud, her world would change for ever. Up to this point, she hadn't mentioned her state to a soul, and she'd been allowing herself time to absorb the news and make her own plans.

She had decided she would need to have her own wishes

firmly in place before meeting Antonio. This was her baby, her body, her life and, while she knew she had a moral obligation to inform him of her pregnancy, she sure as hell wasn't going to let him think he had any right to weigh in on the situation.

'I don't like you,' she said, her eyes locking to his with a defiance that underscored her feelings. 'I think you're cold-hearted, ruthless and manipulative.'

He didn't visibly react, save for a slight tightening around his jaw.

'Go on.'

'You're a Ferrera and I'm part of the diSalvo family, but this is hardly some real-life *Romeo and Juliet* situation. I have no interest in being dragged into a crazy feud that should have ended two generations ago.'

'It is your brother who sought to ruin—'

She lifted a hand to silence him and though he obliged, closing his mouth, his eyes sparked with hers, his impatience obvious.

'He did something. You did something back. What a waste of energy—for both of you!' she denounced scathingly. 'You could have stopped at shoring up your own business interests. But you didn't. Instead of taking the high road, you've sought to ruin him right back. And there's no way I will *ever* be a party to that.'

Antonio's expression tightened further. There was a look of such ruthless determination in his features that many people might have been afraid. Not Amelia. She'd come up against arrogance and cold-hearted ruthlessness before. No, now, she was angry!

'You made this position clear already,' he said finally, the words cold and more heavily accented than usual.

'True. But I feel the need to underscore it.'

'For what purpose?' he demanded. 'Our business together was concluded six weeks ago. There is nothing to be gained from you being here now.'

Her eyes narrowed and for the briefest of moments she thought about leaving. How much easier it would all be if she were to turn on her heel and stalk out of his office, insisting that he never contact her again!

But how could she live with herself? A baby wasn't something you could hide—she was living proof. To know that she'd spent twelve years being raised with her parentage a mystery, that her father had had no idea of her existence. What had they both been denied? Would she have had an actual *family* if her mother had made a different decision?

Memories and past hurts had her straightening her spine, staring at him with renewed intent.

'I'll go soon,' she promised. 'In fact, I'm booked on a flight in a few hours,' she added for good measure, liking the safety and security that fact offered.

His frown was one of non-comprehension. 'You're flying commercial?'

At this, Amelia rolled her eyes. 'As opposed to?'

'DiSalvo Industries has many planes…'

She angled her face away from his. He was right. She could have flown in a private jet, but that wasn't—and never had been—Amelia's style. 'What an environmental nightmare,' she stated disapprovingly. 'Any billionaire gets a whim to go here or there and they power up their own plane, when there are dozens of flights scheduled to that same destination every day.'

'But then you have to fit in with someone else's schedule,' he pointed out with infuriating logic—and despicable arrogance.

'Oh, heaven forbid a little inconvenience.' They were getting off-topic and she didn't particularly want to stand in Antonio's office, arguing the merits of flight timetables with him.

'My schedule allows very little room for flexibility,' he said with an arrogant shrug of his shoulders.

And now Amelia did laugh, just a soft, panicked noise of utter disbelief. 'You're going to hate this, then.' Babies were the very definition of inconvenience, and this one particularly so, given how little either of them could have expected her pregnancy.

'Hate what?' He was wary.

When it came to it, there was no need for any preamble. Like ripping off a Band-Aid, she was simply going to tell him—to get it over with and then go home. With a deep breath and a voice that shook ever so slightly, she said into the silence: 'I'm pregnant, Antonio. And you're the father.'

CHAPTER SIX

'THAT IS IMPOSSIBLE.' His arrogant assertion was the last thing she expected and in other circumstances she might have found that amusing.

'Oh, okay,' she murmured sarcastically. 'Have it your way, then. I'm not pregnant.'

She glared at him, her arms crossed over her body, her expression one of disdain.

'You *can't* be,' he corrected, and Amelia almost felt sorry for him, because Antonio Ferrera didn't strike her as a man who was used to having things happen beyond his control. 'We used protection.'

'Well, you're the only man I've ever slept with and I am most definitely pregnant.' She pinpointed him with an icy glare. 'So I guess it didn't work.'

He was uncharacteristically lost for words.

'Anyway,' she said after a moment's silence, 'I thought you should at least know.' He remained silent. 'But you should also know that I don't need anything from you. I have the financial means to raise this child without worry, and I will be a good mum, all on my own.' She stiffened then, her spine straightening as she forced herself to finish the offer she came willing to extend. 'You may, of course, choose to be involved, if you'd like.' She let that sentiment hit its mark before barrelling forward. 'But I understand why that would be difficult for you and I'm okay—more than okay—with that. This is my baby. You don't have to worry about it.'

'I see.' He seemed to have relocated his voice. He spoke crisply and, though it was a genial enough agreement, it filled Amelia with a sense of wariness because she could feel a 'but' coming. 'And do you think I will let you return to England to have my child? And what, confer upon it your surname? Raise my son or daughter as a diSalvo?'

At that, a surge of anger beat inside her and she pushed at his chest, surprising them both with the violent outburst. 'Don't you dare draft my baby into this damned feud!' she exploded. 'Yes, this child will be a diSalvo because it's *my* child! But I won't be raising it to hate the Ferrera name, so you can relax.'

His expression was one of barely concealed fury.

'And as for you "letting" me do anything, I have a newsflash for you, Antonio. I don't answer to you. I'll leave when I want to leave, and there's not a damned thing you can do about it.'

Her threat was a gauntlet that she really shouldn't have issued. Because he wasn't afraid to run it. Hell, he was relishing the prospect of running it, in fact, and unsettling her attitude of unconcern. As though she could tell him she was pregnant and then waltz out of his life once more! Pregnant, and with his baby.

'You know, there's not even a legal requirement for me to tell you about this,' she continued, apparently oblivious to how close his patience was to fraying.

'And yet you're here,' he snapped.

She opened her mouth and then clamped it shut, before nodding. 'I thought you should know.'

'Thank heavens for small mercies,' he murmured, stalking away from her towards his desk, where he pressed a red button on his phone. 'Cancel my afternoon schedule,' he clipped and then disconnected the call before his assistant could respond.

'You don't need to do that,' Amelia muttered, a hint of panic flaring in her expression now. 'As I said, I'm flying home soon.'

'We have to discuss this,' he murmured, bracing his palms on his desk and dipping his head forward. The reality of this hit him in the solar plexus and a strange metallic taste filled his mouth. Adrenalin. Fight or flight.

He'd tasted it before: when his father had been staring down the barrel of bankruptcy and Antonio had known it was all down to him. That he alone could save his father's legacy: that he alone could salvage the ruins of the once-great Herrera Incorporated.

And he felt that again now. Fight or flight responsibility.

This was his baby, but she was offering him an out. She didn't want him to be involved. She didn't need him.

And God knew he didn't want to have a child. Not now, probably not ever, and sure as hell not with a diSalvo.

But when he lifted his gaze to Amelia, the door to escape swung closed.

Wanted or not, this baby was reality and there was no way he was going to ignore that.

'I intend to raise my child, *querida*,' he said, the words forged from iron.

It was obvious that she had not been expecting that. She took a small step backwards and made a sound of confusion, then shook her head from side to side. 'But…you… Didn't you hear me? You don't have to be involved. You don't need to have anything to do with him.'

'Do you truly believe that? This is my child and, while it is far from ideal that you are to be the mother, it does not change the fact that my flesh and blood is growing in your belly.'

'Gee, thanks. I'm so warm and fuzzy right now,' she clipped.

He ignored her ironic assertion. 'Obviously there is only one solution to this situation.'

'I swear, if you'd said "problem" I would have walked straight out of here.' And then her eyes flew wide and a slim hand lifted to her mouth, covering a gasp. 'You can't be serious?'

'Completely.'

Her face paled—if that was possible, and she staggered back once more. Then a hand came to curve protectively over her still-flat stomach. 'You can't actually expect me to terminate my pregnancy just because you don't want to have a child with a diSalvo?'

Her words seemed to come from a long way away, and took even longer to process. 'What?' he said eventually. And though his English was perfect, he presumed he must have misunderstood something in the translation.

'You want me to have an abortion? How *dare* you? I came here as a courtesy, to tell you that you're going to be a father and that I will allow you to be some part of our child's life and you actually try to bully me into getting rid of our baby?'

She sent one final glare in his direction and then strode purposefully towards the door. She grabbed her bag from a chair as she went and it took Antonio vital seconds to process both her accusation and the certainty that she was about to walk away from him.

He moved quickly, reaching the door first and putting his back against it.

'Move,' she demanded, not meeting his eyes.

And, heaven help him, he knew tears weren't far away for Amelia and he fought a ridiculous urge to comfort her. That was not who or what they were.

'I was not talking about an abortion,' he said in a tone that was carefully wiped clear of emotion.

'Then what exactly did you mean? What "solution" is there to this?'

'We'll get married.'

The relief that had glanced across her features was swallowed by another look of abject panic.

'You're kidding?'

'Do I look like I am kidding?'

'No,' she said, 'but you must be *crazy* if you think I would *ever* marry you.'

'It was not a suggestion,' he said, moving away from the door and returning to his desk.

It was a calculated risk—she would either leave, now he'd given her the opportunity, or she would stay.

And Antonio's instincts, finely honed through his experience in business and trade, told him that she would stay and fight. Because Amelia was not a coward, and she was also not a fool. She might be pregnant with his baby but he held all the trump cards. The perfect bargaining chip to get everything he wanted. Not just their baby, his heir, but Prim'Aqua as well. A primal sense of accomplishment made him want to roar like an animal in the jungle. He pictured his father, pictured all he'd lost, the grief he'd known, and he swept his eyes shut for a moment and simply breathed it in: the certainty that all was about to be righted, once and for all.

'And why is that?' she asked: he'd been right. She wasn't running. She was staying, because she knew as well as he did that this marriage was inevitable.

He took his time, savouring the moment, and then delivered the final blow to her insistence that marriage was a bad idea. 'Because if you don't marry me you know I will destroy your brother once and for all.'

She drew in a sharp breath but then seemed to rally. 'You *wish* you could do that. But you forget, Antonio, I've had time since that night to think, and I've told Carlo about you. He knows what you're up to, and he's not worried.'

'No, he doesn't,' Antonio said simply.

Amelia's eyes narrowed. 'What do you mean?'

'Come and see.'

She glared at him, as though moving close to him was the last thing she wanted.

But Antonio simply loaded up a spreadsheet on his computer and waited with a veneer of patience. Sure enough, a moment later, accompanied by a heavy sigh, Amelia closed the distance between them, pausing just behind him.

'What am I looking at?' she demanded.

'How much of your family's portfolio I have absorbed over the years,' he said, running his own eyes over the spreadsheet with a sense of triumph.

It was all laid out in simple black and white and it painted a stark picture. Several of the companies, if he clicked on them, would show dramatically declining stock prices.

He heard her breathing change, grow faster, and he closed his eyes for a moment before flicking off the computer screen.

In the reflection, his eyes met hers.

'You're saying,' she asked quietly, 'that you'll leave Carlo alone if I marry you?'

Antonio was at a fork in the road. The anger he had felt for a long time was balanced against a child he was determined to raise, and he found he couldn't turn his back on either. 'No,' he said, standing and surprising her by being right there, so close they were almost touching. 'I'm saying that if you marry me and hand over your Prim'Aqua shares, I will leave his remaining businesses alone.'

Indignation shaped her features as the full force of his words sunk in. 'You're blackmailing me?'

He made a sound of disagreement. 'I am offering you a chance to potentially save your brother from financial ruin,' he corrected. 'And I am offering us both a chance to raise our baby as a family, which is, surely, your preference?'

'My preference is never to see you again.'

He arched a thick dark brow. 'Let us stick to the realm of reality, hmm?'

She turned away from him and he fought an urge to lift his fingers to her chin and angle her face back to his. He didn't like it when she hid her expressive face. 'I will *never* give you those shares.'

Determination flashed in the depths of his black eyes. 'Then I will continue to destroy your brother in other ways. And believe me, Amelia, I do nothing by half measures.' He slashed his hand through the air to emphasise his point. 'Already I have wiped half a billion dollars off the value of his business interests—in a little over a month. What do you think I will have achieved by the year's end?'

She drew in a sharp gasp and lifted her face to his. 'You can't be serious?'

'Does it look as though I am joking?'

He was a study in humourless, dark intent.

'But...why?'

'Because I hate him,' he said through gritted teeth. 'And because he deserves this.'

She swept her eyes shut and his gut fired with adrenalin.

'A week after I turned eighteen, I came home from college to discover my father crying.' Sympathy clouded Amelia's expression. 'He'd lost everything—because of your father and your brother. A liquidator had been approached to step in. I honestly believe he wanted to end his life rather than live with the shame of his bankruptcy.'

Pink bloomed in her cheeks. 'I'm sorry he experienced that.'

His eyes lifted to hers, firing with the same strength that had led him then. 'I took over the company that same day. Bit by bit I rebuilt it. It was not easy, *querida,* and it did not happen fast. Every day when I woke up and stared down the barrel of uncertainty and doubt, when I knew my father's life and pride were riding on my success, I swore that I would win. And that I would make your brother pay for what he'd almost done.'

Amelia drew in a sharp breath.

'I hate him.'

'I can see that,' she whispered unevenly. 'But that doesn't give you the right to ruin his life…'

'*He* gave me the right.' Antonio closed his eyes for a moment and he was back in the past, remembering the bleakness in his father's eyes that night, many years earlier.

'He made an enemy of me long ago, and nothing will change that.'

'You talk like this about my brother,' she said stiffly, 'yet you actually expect me to marry you?'

'Yes.' His answer was instantaneous.

'And you'd be happy with the fact you're blackmailing me into it?' she countered, her eyes narrowed. 'You haven't even asked how I'm feeling. You haven't asked about the baby, the due date, nothing! You are heartless and selfish and so damned focused on revenge against my family that you don't even see me as a flesh and blood woman, do you?'

At that, his eyes flared and every cell in his body that was noticing only her womanly self pushed him forward. 'You ask if I see you as a woman?' he demanded fiercely, and now he cupped her cheeks and held her mesmerised face still. His voice was gravelly when he spoke. 'You think I don't want you even now, in the midst of all this?'

Her eyes lowered and he could feel the rushing of her blood; he could see the way she was as affected by this as he.

'That's not what I meant,' she whispered after a moment, but his words were turning her blood into lava. 'You don't see me as a person with my own desires and wants, as someone who deserves to be able to steer her own fate; to make her own decisions.'

'Of course you can decide,' he contradicted gently. 'But one of those choices is better for everyone.'

'Another ultimatum,' she grunted.

He sighed and dropped his hands, walking a few paces clear of her, to where the air was less thick with Amelia-ness and he could think a little straighter.

'Fine,' he said. 'Let us look at this differently. The circumstances of our meeting were unfortunate.'

She snorted her agreement.

'But I am not actually a bad person.'

Her eyes rolled heavenwards and when she spoke her words dripped with scathing sarcasm. 'You're determined to ruin the only family I have.'

'I am *determined*,' he corrected coldly, 'to be a father to this baby. Why can't we create a new family? Yes, I'm a Herrera and you're a diSalvo, but we are also a mother and a father now. I want us to live together and to raise this baby side by side, giving it everything we can in life. Tell me this is not what you want, Amelia. Tell me you don't want our child to grow up with a loving mother and father always at hand.'

The words were dangerous because they were so, so achingly true.

Her own childhood flashed before her eyes. The absence of any kind of family structure or regular home, the absence of time and love and affection. A mother who saw Amelia at times as an inconvenience and at others as a pet, and eventually an accessory, when Amelia was old enough, at eleven, to be dragged to parties that were, in hindsight, woefully inappropriate for a girl on the cusp of womanhood.

The things Amelia saw at her mother's side! The drugged-out state of various guests, the orgies, spectacular fist fights. More than once she'd had to call an ambulance when someone had become so high they were a danger to themselves or others. Then there were the nightclubs, when Penny would park Amelia with the bouncers and she'd listen to them swearing and ogling women all night—it was a wonder she'd reached adulthood with any semblance of normality.

In the midst of it all, she had desperately wanted someone who would just be *average. Boring.* Someone who would read her books and make her pasta for dinner, who would take her to the playground or on long walks, who would ask her about *her* life, her hopes, her dreams.

She had wanted a mother—and *not* a mother like Penny.

And oh, how she'd craved a father. In her mind, she'd probably idealised what role a father might take. Her knowledge had been fleshed out from the pages of her books, but she'd imagined a sort of Mr Bennet type figure, benevolent and kindly, strict when necessary.

And Antonio? What kind of father would he be to their baby?

'We hate each other,' she said quietly, trying to remind herself of all the reasons this marriage was a stupid idea. 'No child should grow up in a house where two parents can't stand one another.'

'We have more than seven months to find a way to co-exist,' he said sensibly. 'I think we can achieve that.'

'And if we can't?'

His eyes glittered with determination. 'I do not see failure as an option here, *hermosa*.'

Frustration curdled inside her. 'It would never work.'

'You cannot say that with any certainty.'

'Oh, yes, I can,' she insisted. 'You're the last man on

earth I would ever choose to marry, and it's quite clear the feeling is mutual.'

'This marriage wouldn't be about us, though,' he said simply. 'It's about giving our child a family from the moment of his birth...'

Something else occurred to Amelia and it had her fixing Antonio with a stone-cold stare. 'You just want him to have your name, don't you?' she demanded.

'Of course that matters to me.' Antonio shrugged, and she was torn between despising his motivation and admiring his honesty. 'But I would insist on his taking my name, married or not.'

She let out a sigh of exasperation. 'God, you're an old-fashioned, patriarchal jerk.'

'Perhaps,' he said with a lift of his shoulders. 'But I am also a man who wants to marry you, and I think you should think very carefully about the situation you find yourself in.'

'No way.' She shook her head but the words lacked conviction.

He moved towards the door and wrenched it inwards, his eyes holding hers with steely determination. 'Think about it,' he said simply, as though he was asking what she'd like for dinner, or which was her favourite song.

'I don't need to think about it,' she insisted, walking towards the door and pausing when she drew level with him. 'I know my answer.'

'Then think about what happens if you don't marry me.' He moved closer. 'Think about what happens if you make an enemy of me.' And, because he couldn't help himself, he leaned down and whispered into her ear, 'And think about the silver lining of a marriage between us, *querida*. Night after night in my bed as my wife...'

His words chased her all the way home, rattling around inside her shocked head. In a million years, and not for a

million pounds, would she have thought Antonio Herrera
would suggest marriage. He wasn't the marrying kind! And
he clearly had major issues with her family! Surely it was
the last thing he *wanted*.

Him? What about her?

She'd run as fast as she could from the kind of life he
lived and she didn't regret that decision. Not for a moment.
To marry a man like him and be swept up in his world—
she'd regret it.

And yet...this baby! *Their* baby. This baby was as much
his as it was hers. She had no interest in trying to pretend
that wasn't the case.

This baby wasn't hypothetical. It was an actual being,
a little person who would be a part of her life before she
knew it. And she didn't want to look back on her baby's childhood and wish she'd done more, given him or
her more. She didn't want him to feel lonely, as she had.
Scared, abandoned, worried—she wanted this baby to have
everything!

She wanted perfection—she wanted a fairy tale, but that
was never going to be her future.

Her thoughts became a screaming choir in the background of her life. Every morning she woke with visions
of Antonio filling her mind, and she heard him all day—
his suggestion of marriage, his insistence that it would be
best for their baby.

But she remembered his rage too. His hatred for her
brother and father. His insistence that their families' feud
was still very much an ongoing affair.

So when Carlo called one evening, clearly drunk and
upset, she knew what it would be about even before he'd
spoken.

'Jesus Christ!' he spat down the line, and then hurled
several more expletives in fiery Italian. 'That bastard's
done a number on me, Amelia. He's got his hands on *ev-*

erything! He's going to absolutely *ruin* me! Why didn't I realise?'

Because Antonio is very, very good at what he does, Amelia responded inwardly, her eyes swept shut as, for the millionth time since leaving Madrid, she conjured an image of the Spaniard in her mind's eye, and her body reacted predictably.

Night after night in my bed as my wife...

His words made her pulse speed up and her heart race, even now, a week after he'd whispered them like a sexy caress against her ear.

'How am I going to tell Dad I let this happen?'

Her heart sank because the plaintive note in his voice was the only thing that could have brought her to her knees. For twelve years she hadn't known she had a brother or a father, but then she'd turned up on their doorstep and they'd taken her in. They'd loved her, accepted her, and been the closest thing to a 'normal' family she'd ever known. What wouldn't she do to repay them that kindness? What wouldn't she do to protect them from this kind of grief and worry?

She soothed Carlo as best she could, placating him with hollow promises, and all the while her own future sharpened before her eyes.

When she disconnected the call some time later, Carlo was calmer but her own insides were quivering with emotion.

There was also a kernel of strength. She was resolute.

Because the answer to all her concerns was staring her in the face and she could—and would—be brave enough to admit that.

She could marry Antonio and she could give their child a family and a home, and the stability she'd never, ever had. She could give their baby the start in life she wanted, and that he or she deserved.

And she could solve Carlo's worries for good. At least she thought she could.

She would marry Antonio, but only if he agreed to her rules. Because Amelia diSalvo wasn't a fool, and Antonio was going to learn that the hard way…

CHAPTER SEVEN

'TWICE IN ONE WEEK—lucky me,' he murmured, crossing the marble floor of the foyer, his eyes fixed on Amelia diSalvo. As with the last time she'd come to his office in Madrid, she'd dressed to impress, this time in a pair of white trousers and a simple silk camisole top, pale blue in colour. Gold bangles covered one wrist, so many that they ran towards her elbows. Her skin had the hint of a tan and her face was sparingly made-up. He took his time studying her appearance, not least because he sensed her impatience and enjoyed provoking that reaction in her.

'Antonio—' her voice was clipped, her eyes cold with a silent warning '—can we speak?'

He tilted his head in silent agreement and gestured with his hand towards his office. She shot him one last look, a wary appraisal and a warning all wrapped into one, and then she walked ahead of him, just like the last time she'd been here.

As he passed his secretary he said, 'Hold my calls. No interruptions.'

'Yes, sir.'

Yes, sir. That was the response he was accustomed to. He spoke and people listened. His suggestions were universally obeyed because his suggestions made sense. Because he knew what he was doing. Because he was Antonio Herrera.

That seemed to hold little sway with Amelia, however. She didn't wait on the threshold of his office this time. She pushed the door open and walked inside, so that when he joined her she was pouring two glasses of water.

'I take it you've reconsidered my proposal,' he murmured and she jerked her face towards his, her eyes zipping with resentment and anger.

'I've reconsidered it and reconsidered it again a thousand times,' she muttered. 'In fact, right now I'm wondering what the hell I'm doing here.'

He waited. There were times for arguing and convincing, and there were times for simply being silent and letting a person explain their mindset. This was a time for the latter.

'*If* we were to get married…' she said

Something in his chest heaved with relief. No—not relief. It was a sense of victory that flared in his gut, because she was going to agree with his suggestion after all. This was her own version of *Yes, sir.*

'I would have some rules.'

'I see,' he murmured, unconcerned. The war was about to be won—so what if there were final skirmishes? 'Go on.'

She nodded, but there was anxiety in her features. 'This wouldn't be a normal marriage,' she said, a small frown creasing her brow. 'We don't like each other. We don't even know each other. But if the whole purpose of it is to give our child a family, we'd have to…redress that.'

He was silent.

'I mean, we would need to get to know one another—make an effort to be civil.'

That was simple enough. He nodded his agreement.

Her eyes narrowed, and he saw something beyond her anxiety. A steeliness that he hadn't expected.

'And, to that end, you'd need to give up whatever you're doing with Carlo's business interests.'

His eyes narrowed imperceptibly and danger whipped through the air. 'I will not do that.'

'Then I can't marry you,' she said firmly, crossing her arms over her chest in a classic gesture of rejection. 'So we might as well start talking about custody.'

He held a hand up, his nostrils flaring. 'You would honestly be happy to give up without even trying?'

He noticed the way his accusation landed; she winced, her face scrunching up, and she looked away from him. 'I'm here, aren't I?'

A familiar rush of victory throbbed inside Antonio. 'Yes.'

'But I can't marry a man who hates my brother and my father. They're—' her voice cracked unexpectedly '—they're important to me.'

He couldn't help the snort of derision. 'So much so you change your name and hide from them in England?'

'I'm not hiding from them!' she retorted swiftly. 'I'm… living my own life. And is it any wonder? With men like you waiting for me as part of the diSalvo legacy?'

He ground his teeth together, refusing to analyse why her words bothered him. 'Fine. You love them. I hate them. That doesn't matter.' He slashed his hand through the air. 'Our baby is separate to that.'

Her expression was pure exasperation. 'Our baby is separate to that? You can't seriously—'

'What?' he demanded, waiting for her to finish her sentence.

'You're like a child,' she snapped, lifting her fingertips to her temple and rubbing.

He might have laughed were it not for how ludicrous her statement was. No one had ever called him childish. Even when he was a child!

'Careful, *querida*, or I might be tempted to remind you of how very adult I can be…'

He was rewarded by a hint of a blush spreading through her cheeks. 'That won't be necessary.' The words were so clipped and cold, yet he smiled. A wolfish smile, because he could see the fine tremble in her knees and the flush of her cheeks and he knew that whatever had drawn them together in the first instance was still electrifying the air between them.

'I won't raise a baby in an environment of hate.'

'Then let's not hate one another,' he proposed.

'You know what I mean,' she said, shaking her head so pale blonde hair flew around her shoulders, catching the afternoon sunlight in a way that made him think of the beach and lazy afternoons on the deck of his yacht. 'My father and brother will be a part of this child's life.'

That, he hadn't considered and the suggestion was immediately unwelcome.

'What's the baby's first birthday going to be like, with you and Carlo glaring at one another across the cake?'

'We shall have two parties.' He shrugged, as though her concern was really so easily solved.

She rolled her eyes, a habit he should have been bothered by but instead found strangely addictive. 'So you're just going to pretend my family don't exist?'

'I didn't say that,' he responded instantly.

'Oh, of course!' She slapped her palm to her forehead in an exaggerated gesture of recollection. 'You're going to be busy eviscerating them financially.'

He shrugged. 'What I do with my business has nothing to do with our child. He will not be affected by this.'

'So you won't raise him to hate all diSalvos, as you were raised?'

'I was *not* raised to hate your family,' he ground out. 'Your brother almost broke my father. Your brother, your father. This is their doing.'

'Fine,' she snapped, crossing her arms once more. 'They started it. So you can still be the bigger person and walk away.'

He narrowed his eyes. 'It's too late for that.'

She opened her mouth to say something but he shook his head, lifting a hand into the air to silence her.

'Marry me. Marry me because you want to give our child a stable family. Marry me because you know it is the right thing to do.'

She swallowed, biting into her lower lip and turning away from him, pacing over towards the windows. Madrid glistened in the distance, and her shoulders slumped forward a little as she—apparently—lost herself in contemplation. Seeing her weakening, realising he could push home his advantage, he took a step closer.

'You didn't know your father until you were a teenager. True?'

He knew it was—he'd read the file his investigator had put together.

'Yes.'

Antonio's expression tightened and something heavy landed in his gut. He'd known about his own child for a week and already he couldn't imagine what kind of man he would have to be to neglect him or her like that.

'And didn't you wish he'd been more involved in your life?' he pushed, watching the way her features visibly contracted, showing pain and hurt.

'There's no sense wishing for what's not possible,' she said with a shrug. It was an imitation of nonchalance, he could tell. He wished she'd turn to face him so he could see her eyes, see her mouth, see all of her.

'But I knew my father,' Antonio continued, his voice thick with unexpected emotion—the loss was still fresh, he supposed. 'He was a busy man but he always made time for me. He talked to me each evening, telling me stories, and on weekends we went hiking through the forest that surrounded our home. We fished in a stream and ran until our lungs threatened to burst. When I was little, if I had a nightmare, it was my father who comforted me. He was an excellent man.'

Amelia turned to face him and her eyes were like the ocean on a turbulent day. 'Why are you telling me this?'

'Because you should know what kind of father I intend to be for our child.'

Her eyes swept shut, her long silky lashes forming perfect fans against the pearly whiteness of her cheeks.

'Don't you want our child to have that?'

Her expression showed anguish when she opened her eyes, blinking to face him. 'Yes.'

He admired her for not prevaricating, and he admired her even more when she visibly pulled herself together, extinguishing the flames of anguish and assuming an expression of calm.

'Yes, I do,' she agreed more firmly, as though she were convincing herself. 'But I can't marry a man intent on destroying my family. That's obvious.'

He understood her need to negotiate on this point, but Antonio wasn't a man to give concessions. Not when it came to getting what he wanted. In a battle of wills with Amelia he would back himself every time. 'Then give me Prim'Aqua. Agree to marry me.'

'And you'll stop going after Carlo's other businesses?' she whispered, the words haunted.

He looked at her long and hard and finally nodded. 'For now.'

She frowned. 'What does that mean?'

'Only that I expect you to try to make our marriage work,' he said. 'If you don't, if you walk away from me, then the deal is off.'

Her breathing was raspy and shallow. 'You're serious?'

'Deadly.'

Her complexion paled.

'I am the father of your child, and I want to marry you.

I want the marriage to be a success because I am not used to failure, *querida*. This is what I want. What is it that you want? What matters most to you?'

Amelia blanched, his ultimatum horrifying because she already knew that she was going to agree. She pressed a hand over her stomach, and her heart squeezed at the thought of the little life growing inside her. Would it be a boy? Or a girl?

She didn't care—she just wanted a healthy, happy baby.

She turned away from Antonio—looking at him made it almost impossible to think straight—and paced towards the window. The same Gaudí was peeking back at her, this time bathed in gentle sunshine.

Antonio hated the diSalvo family, and the same could be said of Carlo and the Herreras. But her child wouldn't feel that bitterness. This child had the power to heal those breaches. Surely once their baby was born, and was an actual little person rather than a hypothetical concept, Antonio would see for himself how damaging it was to continue this ridiculous blood feud? Surely he'd wish to put paid to the last vestiges of resentment, for the sake of their child?

It was a gamble.

Because he hadn't said or done anything to give her the impression that his attitude might soften. But was it possible that over time, and as he got to know her, he would see the futility in hating Carlo the way he did? Particularly when the object of his acrimony was his own child's relatives.

She spun around, her eyes pinning him, her gaze unknowingly forceful. 'Promise me you'll…be reasonable,' she said instead.

His brows lifted upwards. 'I'm always reasonable.'

She made a scoffing noise of disbelief. 'I'm serious, Antonio.'

'As am I.'

Amelia shook her head. 'This is ridiculous. There's been nothing reasonable about how you've behaved with me. Nothing. You're the most intractable, difficult…'

'Bastard, yes, you've said this.'

She ground her teeth together. 'I'm not going to be trapped into a marriage that makes me miserable, and so far you've done nothing to show me that you're the kind of man I can even vaguely bear to be around.'

His expression was pure sensual challenge and it had the desired result. Her pulse notched up a gear and her breath burned in her lungs.

She pushed on before he could speak. 'You're asking me to marry you and stay married to you, and you're giving me nothing in return.'

'I am giving you,' he said so softly it was dangerous, 'an assurance that I will leave your brother's other business interests alone. And, believe me, Amelia, this is not a concession I make easily.'

She *could* believe it. In that moment, she felt his hatred and rage and she wondered how he'd managed to conceal those emotions so well when he'd come to the cottage.

It was so far from ideal! If only there was a way she could wrest some control back from him—show him that she wasn't going to be pushed around. 'I won't sign my shares of Prim'Aqua over to you,' she said quietly, 'until the baby is born.'

He frowned, his expression showing he didn't fully comprehend the distinction.

'Why the delay?'

'Because—' she spoke slowly, logically '—once I give you Prim'Aqua, you hold all the cards. Even if I do decide to divorce you.' She tilted her chin defiantly. 'And I will not stay with you unless I truly believe that our marriage is in the best interests of the baby. Understood?'

It was obvious from his expression that he hadn't expected a challenge on this point. He was cool and calm again almost instantly, but for a moment she saw surprise flare in his expression. What she didn't register was the look of grudging admiration. 'Fine,' he said, shrugging with apparent indifference. 'Seven months is not so long to wait.'

'And you won't touch my brother's businesses in the meantime,' she demanded, waving a single finger in the air to underscore her point. The silk of her camisole strained across her chest, emphasising the gentle curves there, so Antonio's eyes momentarily dropped lower. 'Swear you'll leave Carlo alone.'

Antonio's jaw clenched and he slowly drew his eyes back to hers in a way that set her pulse racing. 'You do not trust that I want to do what is in our child's best interests?' he asked after a moment. 'You are not the only one making a sacrifice here, *querida*. Believe it or not, marrying you is the last thing I would have wanted.'

'Gee, thanks,' she drawled sarcastically.

'Marrying *anyone*,' he corrected with a shrug of his broad shoulders.

'That makes it so much better.' She couldn't help rolling her eyes, but frustration and impotence were burning through her.

'You came to me today,' he reminded her after a moment. 'And I believe we have discussed what we are each willing to give to make this work. So? What is your decision, Amelia?'

'I…' What was the conclusion to that sentence? He was right: she'd come to his office today, and with every intention of marrying him. And, while she desperately wanted Carlo to be immune from this man's vengeance, there was a far greater consideration.

Their baby deserved the very best. Materially, she could provide everything the child needed, but what of that gaping hole in the middle of Amelia's heart, from her own child-hood? What of her own desperate yearning for a father?

Her eyes landed on Antonio's face, his devilishly hand-some face, and she expelled a soft, slow breath. And then, with every sense that she was making a deal with the devil, she nodded. 'Fine. I'll marry you.'

There was a momentary response of triumph, a flare of reaction in his jet-black eyes, and then he moved on, with that rapier-sharp mind he was renowned for.

'You'll move to Madrid?'

Amelia blinked. She was still processing the monumen-tal agreement she'd just entered into and he was already firing onto the next point of negotiation, without giving her so much as a moment to breathe.

'But… I live in England. I have a job…' she pointed out, but weakly, more weakly than she would have liked. Damn it, this was supposed to be on her terms and he was push-ing all her buttons to get what he wanted.

'The same could be said for me.'

She bit down on her lip, swallowing past a lump of un-certainty. Her whole world was about to change—she was having a baby. Fighting change was going to get her pre-cisely nowhere. Leaving her job was inevitable—did it make a difference if that was in six months or now? From the perspective of the children she was teaching, it would be better for them to have a new teacher at the start of the year rather than halfway through.

She could leave her job—temporarily. But to move to Madrid?

She'd run a mile from this very world he inhabited.

Her time in Italy, as a diSalvo, had been harrowing. She thought of the women who'd befriended her as a teen-ager, using her as a way to get to her brother. The 'friends' who'd only been jealous—one in particular who'd got Ame-lia drunk and then taken unflattering photographs of her passed out and shared them across social media. Men who'd seen her as a new, shiny toy on their society scene and done whatever they could to get her into bed. Only she'd learned her lesson from Penny: Amelia was no one's plaything.

And marriage? Marriage to a man like this? How many of the men who'd flirted with her and tried to tempt her to become their mistress had been married? Was that the kind of future she had in store? Marriage to a man like Antonio, but marriage in name only?

She'd run a mile from this world, and with very good reason. Her time in Italy had been miserable. And though she'd loved her father and brother, they couldn't see that the way they lived wasn't something she wanted any part of. They couldn't see how ill suited she was for that lifestyle.

Her eyes swept shut as she thought of the life she'd carved out for herself and felt it disappearing from her, like a ship sinking into a silent, deathly ocean.

Perhaps her distress showed in her face because he was suddenly solicitous. 'You will like Madrid, *hermosa*.'

'It's not about Madrid,' she said frankly, worrying at her lower lip.

'Then what is it?'

How could she tell him? To admit vulnerabilities to a man like Antonio was to give him a weapon with which to wound her. And she was smarter than that!

'It's just a lot to ask of me,' she covered awkwardly. 'Particularly when you aren't even willing to consider moving to the UK.'

'I cannot do my work from the middle of nowhere,' he said simply.

'And what of my work?' She couldn't resist asking, though she'd already made her peace with the sense of leaving her job sooner rather than later.

'You are going to have to stop working at some point,'

he said with infuriating logic—as though six months was the same as six days! 'Why not now?'

'Because I love my job,' she said, aware that she was being stubborn purely for the sake of it. She expelled a sigh and ran a hand through her hair, not noticing the way his eyes followed the simple gesture as though transfixed. 'But I will think about it.'

His eyes glowed. 'Good. Then it is done.'

Amelia blinked rapidly. 'What's done?'

He walked away from her, towards his desk, and retrieved something, then a moment later was standing in front of her. 'Our engagement.' He reached for her hand and she was too shell-shocked to react. He put something in it and she looked down to see a small velvet box. She flipped it open on autopilot and couldn't help the small sound of admiration that escaped her lips at the sight of the ring.

An enormous turquoise gem, square-shaped, sat in the centre and it was surrounded by sparkling white diamonds on each side, so that it glistened and shone. The band was platinum and there were delicate swirls on either side.

'It's beautiful,' she said with a frown, because it was so much lovelier and more elegant than she would have credited Antonio with choosing.

He made a gruff noise of agreement then slid it onto her finger. They both stared down at it, and she was mesmerised by the sight of it on her finger.

'It was my grandmother's,' he said after a moment. 'She had eyes like yours.'

Amelia blinked at this reference to his forebear, as it reminded her obliquely of the feud that lay between them.

She didn't want to think about it in that moment. It was hardly a romantic marriage proposal, but it was still a proposal and she would have preferred it not to be tainted by talk of the animosity that flowed between their families.

'Thank you.' She frowned. It was hardly an appropriate sentiment—he'd blackmailed her into this marriage, no two ways about it.

'I've had the papers drawn and a judge has offered a special dispensation. Our marriage can take place within a week. I presume that's long enough for you to wrap things up in England?'

'You make it sound like finishing a meal, not resigning my job and shutting up my house.'

'I know it is more complex than that, and yet I would prefer to be married as soon as possible.' And with a sigh, and as though the words were being dragged from him against his will, 'If your employer requires more notice, then I suppose you could return once we are married. We could stay in your house *for a time*, if we must.'

'Gee, great,' she said with an upward shift of her eyes. 'Seeing as you're clearly so willing…'

He interrupted her, his words spoken with the same strength as a blade of steel. 'I am willing to do what it takes to make you my wife.'

She swallowed, the intensity of his statement almost robbing her of breath. This was about possession, she reminded herself, nothing more. Possession, ownership, control. He wanted their baby: she came with it.

She couldn't have said why the thought was unpalatable to her. 'Do you just have engagement rings sitting in your desk drawer on the off-chance a woman might drop by?'

His eyes smouldered when they met hers. 'I got it from the family vault the day after you left Madrid.'

'Why?'

'Because I knew you'd be back.'

She made a groaning noise in acknowledgement of that. 'What if you'd been wrong?'

He caught her hand and ran his fingertips lightly over the ring. 'Then I would have come to England and helped you see sense,' he said, the words simple, light, and yet a shiver of anticipation and adrenalin coursed through her veins.

Was she seeing sense? Or had she moved into the realm of insanity by agreeing to this?

Amelia couldn't say: only time would tell.

Antonio stared at his desk, his expression brooding.

It was all laid out before him: the totality of his aggressive investment in diSalvo Industries, the way he'd been slowly, meticulously devaluing them, ruining them for the sake of destruction alone. Businesses that had little interest to him beyond one aspect: their ability to wound Carlo and Giacomo.

His fiancée's family.

I can't marry a man intent on destroying my family.

And yet she was, and he was. Destroying the diSalvos had obsessed him for so long, and now, since his father's death, it had become his reason for being.

For so long, he had planned it: he would take what he could from them, and he would enjoy standing over them, seeing the shock on their faces when they realised how completely he'd masterminded their downfall.

He'd thought Prim'Aqua was the sum total of what he wanted, but now there was Amelia. Was it possible that in marrying her, creating a family with her, raising the child as the Herrera heir, he held the greatest key to destroying them?

Carlo hated Antonio—just as Antonio hated Carlo. So what would this child's existence do to the diSalvos? His smile was one of dark pleasure. It would destroy them, that was what. They would possibly even believe that Antonio had planned it—the seduction, the pregnancy—planned it all. His grin spread. And wouldn't that kill them? They'd hate it.

So much the better.

A light on his phone blinked, signalling a call, but he ignored it.

Amelia would be on a flight by now. His brows knitted into a gesture of silent disdain at her insistence that she fly commercial—yet again. To his disbelief, she hadn't even booked first class.

It was clear that she was engaged in some kind of protest against her wealth and situation, but to ignore all the luxuries she had at her disposal, and then the luxuries that he could furnish her with, beggared belief.

Then again, didn't everything about this situation?

Sleeping with her had been a mistake. A beautiful, heavenly mistake. Because, while the sex had been unforgettable, he'd returned to Madrid knowing he *had* to forget her. He had to put that misstep in the past and refocus his attention on his need to avenge the insults inflicted on his father.

And he'd been doing that, destroying the diSalvos and relishing his success.

But her pregnancy... He frowned, thinking of the unlikelihood of that. He was religious about using contraceptives. He was no monk. Sex was a part of his life, and he knew children weren't on his wish list. But the second Amelia had dropped her bombshell he'd felt an explosion of protective instincts, a primal, all-encompassing need to do whatever he could for that child.

That it was a child he would be raising with a diSalvo was something he would have to accept.

That had nothing to do with business—what he and Amelia shared, the life they would make for their baby, was all personal.

CHAPTER EIGHT

'*I NOW PRONOUNCE you husband and wife.*'

The words swum around Amelia's mind, heavily accented, and ever so slightly like a death knell.

Only that was stupid and dramatic. She was no little lamb, being led to the slaughter. She'd chosen this marriage, and she had to remember that. She wasn't a piece of detritus being drawn into an ocean's current—she had gone to Antonio and told him of her pregnancy, and she had chosen to at least try to create a life with him.

A real life?

Anxiety gnawed at the edges of her stomach as she came to the crux of the question that was tormenting her.

What exactly did a 'real' marriage look like, to Antonio Herrera?

She barely knew him, she thought, sliding a sideways glance to the man beside her. He drove the car through the streets of Madrid with effortless ease, the afternoon sunshine warm and golden, the powerful car eating up the distance between the utilitarian courthouse in which they'd said their vows and...

And what?

His home.

Another thing she had no idea about. Would it be a luxurious penthouse? A mansion? A yacht? Trepidation at the unquestionable glamour and luxury that awaited her had her remembering the life she'd fled, a life she'd sworn she'd never return to. Yet here she was: as far from her life as a primary school teacher as it was possible to be.

He wore a tuxedo and she wore a dress—simple, white, no lace, no pearls, no beading, no zips. The only concession to the fact it was a wedding was a little bouquet of white roses Antonio had presented her with when the limousine had brought her, straight from the airport, to the town hall. To any passers-by they might have even looked like a normal couple, sneaking off to quickly marry, happy at the prospect of the future that awaited them.

But this was far more like a business arrangement than anything else.

So who exactly had she got into bed with? No, not bed! Her cheeks infused with pink heat and she focused her gaze on the city streets as they passed.

He was ruthless, if his behaviour towards Carlo was anything to go by. But then, there were his charitable works—was that just an excuse, though, to soften his reputation as a hard-hearted bastard? Good PR work, the strings being pulled by an agency focused on rehabilitating his image rather than being motivated by any genuine social concern?

It was hard to believe Antonio particularly cared about his image, or how people might perceive him.

And it was better for her to believe that the man who would be a father to her child had good in his heart, somewhere.

I am not actually a bad person, he'd said, right before suggesting this marriage.

A marriage you agreed to, her memory pointed out sharply.

Her eyes dropped to her finger, and the rings she wore now. A simple diamond band accompanied the engagement ring, sparkling back at her encouragingly.

'Having regrets?' The words surprised her. They hadn't spoken in at least thirty minutes, since leaving the town hall.

She angled her face towards his and wished she hadn't when she found his eyes momentarily scanning her. Only for a scant few seconds, then his attention was claimed by the road, but it was enough. Heat seared her, expectation lurched in her gut and memories—oh, the memories! The way he'd kissed her, the way it had felt for his lips to press against hers, the urgency of their lovemaking, as though each had been waiting for the other all their lives. What madness had driven them into bed?

'Because it is too late to change your mind, you know,' he said, a tight smile stretching across his too-handsome face, the expression shoving more pleasurable thoughts from her mind.

'Not at all.'

'So you have been twisting your fingers to shreds because you are relaxed?' he responded with scepticism.

Had she been? It was a nervous gesture she'd had since childhood: lacing her fingers over and over as worries tumbled through her mind. She'd thought she'd conquered it but old habits, apparently, died hard.

'I'm thinking about our marriage,' she said honestly. 'And about the fact I know very little about my husband.'

He turned to face her again, slowing down at traffic lights.

'And what I do know,' she said quietly, 'I don't like, at all.'

His expression was one of grim mockery. 'I'm a big, bad Herrera,' he pointed out. 'Of course you do not like me.'

'It has nothing to do with this ridiculous feud,' she returned. 'I had no idea about that when we slept together; I hadn't even heard of you, except for an occasional mention in the papers.' Her teeth dug into her lower lip. 'This is all about your behaviour. To my brother, my father—your attitude to my family, and now me...'

'And what is my attitude to you?' he enquired, looking back at the road and easing the car into gear when the lights changed to green. The city had given way without her realising it, and now there was green on either side and he slowed as they approached a large gate. It flashed as the car neared and swung open, allowing Antonio to drive through.

She didn't answer that. It was hard to pinpoint what was bothering her, when actually he hadn't done anything but argue for this marriage. And she had understood his reasoning, had even agreed with him. But she knew why she'd done this—she wanted to give their baby everything she'd never had.

Why had he married her? Was it something so simple, and barbaric, as insisting that their child have his surname? He'd claimed that was a part of it, but what else was there?

Many possibilities came to mind; none of them relaxed her.

At the base of all her worries was the likelihood that Antonio saw this baby as yet another pawn in his war with her family, and there was worry there—worry that he might end up hurting the child. That her hopes for this baby having stability and love would be destroyed by his need for vengeance. And what would she do then?

A sigh escaped her lips without approval. She didn't see the answering look of impatience that crossed his face: her attention was captured by the view they drove past.

On one side of the car, heavenly grass and enormous oak trees spread for miles, with a lake at the centre. On the other? Mansions. Enormous, palatial homes with tall fences, stretches of darkly tinted glass, infinity pools, landscaped lawns.

She knew the drill.

She compressed her lips, disapproval filling her body.

Of course he lived somewhere like this.

Only his house wasn't one of the homes lined up in a fancy row, overlooking the park. His house was *in* the park. What she'd taken to be a public area was, in fact, part of Antonio's garden. The house itself was like a twenty-first century palace—all white walls and blue glass, with sharp lines and bright flowers tumbling out of terracotta pots on the endless balconies.

It was beautiful, she admitted grudgingly to herself. 'If you think we're raising our child in this museum, you're crazy,' was what she said. And when he drew the car to a halt at the front of the mansion she continued to stare at it.

'What's wrong with it?' he asked, the words flattened of emotion.

'Well, for one thing, look at the terraces. Do you have any idea how risky that is?'

His tone was curt. 'Yes, if only there were some handy way to keep children off terraces. I don't know, something flat that could be pulled to create a barrier. Something a bit like, oh, what's the word for it...a door?'

She scowled. 'Sarcasm doesn't suit you.'

He laughed then, a husky sound. 'And pettiness doesn't suit you. The house is fine, and you know it, so stop complaining for the sake of it and come and have a look.'

Only the fact he'd stepped out of the car and was coming around to her side had her pushing the door open and making a hasty exit before he could open the door for her. It was symbolic of the marriage she wanted—separate, but together. She nodded to herself at that description. It was perfect.

Marriage didn't mean they had to know everything about one another. Courtesy, civility, distance.

That could work, right?

Only his look showed he knew exactly what she was doing and she was left with a sense of having acted childishly, and she hated that! Her fingers knotted together before she realised what she was doing.

'The house itself is gated,' he pointed out, 'so there is little worry our children would find their way into the lake.'

'Children?' She stopped walking, pressing a flat hand against her stomach. 'This is one baby, so far as we know.'

He shrugged. 'So far.'

'You mean...?' She gaped. 'We aren't having more children.'

He gestured towards the house. 'Lots of rooms to fill...'

'That's a great reason to compound this situation,' she muttered, to cover the way her heart had speeded up at the very idea of a big, happy, noisy family—with this man.

'You want to give our child everything, don't you? Does that not include siblings?'

She stared at him, her eyes sparking. 'No.' Not if it means sleeping with you again, she added inwardly, but her traitorous body surged at the very idea and she spun away from him to hide her reaction. The dress was a fine cotton and her nipples were hardening at the mere thought of being possessed by him once more.

'We'll see.' He simply shrugged and the hand he placed at the small of her back might have been intended only to guide her forward, but her body was already on fire, her pulse racing, spurred on by memories of that night, so that she was electrified by the simple touch.

But pride held her steady; she wouldn't give him the satisfaction of knowing how he affected her by jerking out of his reach.

'The door opens with a code,' he said, tapping in some numbers. 'Raul will programme yours.'

'Raul?'

'Head of my security and operations.'

'You have security?'

He shot her a look of impatience. 'Yes, *querida*.'

'What the heck does someone like you need a bodyguard for? You're six and a half feet of muscle. Are you telling me you couldn't defend yourself?'

His smile showed both amusement and something else, something darker and more dangerous, because it spoke of a desire in his bloodstream that answered her own.

She blinked it away.

'Raul is not a bodyguard,' he said with a shake of his head. 'His purview is the security of my properties, the safety of my staff, and protecting my cyber interests. He monitors the alarms, ensures staff are vetted appropriately. And he will oversee your protection as well, from now on.'

'I don't need protection.'

'Amelia—' He expelled a heavy breath, clicking the door shut behind them. It was impossible not to contrast this phenomenal space with the cosiness of Bumblebee Cottage. They were standing inside a door now, as they had been then but, instead of quaint lighting and pictures drawn by her students, here there was all white marble, high ceilings, crystal chandeliers and world-famous pieces of art hanging from the walls. Mondrian, Dali and—of course—Picasso. She stared at the bright modernist piece with a growing sense of awe.

'Amelia?' he repeated. 'Are you okay?'

She blinked, her nausea nothing to do with the baby in that moment so much as the enormity of what she'd done. Marriage to Antonio was one thing, but until she'd stepped into his lavish home and been confronted with the sight of millions of pounds' worth of artwork within the hallway alone, she hadn't completely grasped what she was doing: the world she was moving back into.

'I'm fine,' she lied. 'Just hot.' And it *was* a hot day, stiflingly so, but the house itself was perfectly climate controlled. Other urges were responsible for the heat that ran rampant through her veins…

'Come, have a seat,' he urged, gesturing deeper into the house. Three steps led down into a sunken living space that showed views of the park they'd driven alongside. The windows were floor to ceiling and several of them slid to open completely, so that the enormous terrace beyond could become a part of this room with ease.

The sofas were white leather, large and soft. She sank into one and wished she hadn't because it was comfortable and she didn't want to be at ease. She needed to keep her wits about her.

Antonio disappeared, then returned a moment later with a bottle of ice-cold water. 'Drink this,' he said, handing it to her.

'Yes, sir,' she couldn't resist clipping back, diminishing his act of concern to one of dictatorialism.

He crouched down in front of her and, God help her, her eyes fell to his powerful haunches and the way the fabric of his trousers strained across them. He'd discarded his jacket somewhere, presumably in the kitchen or wherever he'd pulled the water bottle from, so her eyes roamed upwards, to the flat tightness of his stomach and, finally, up to his face. He was watching her but his expression gave little away.

'Do you have any idea how much you're worth?'

The question surprised her. She brushed it aside. 'Not precisely.'

He arched a brow, as though he couldn't believe this, and then shook his head. 'A small fortune. No, a *large* fortune. You were worth millions of pounds before you married me, and now? Do you not see that there is *some* risk you have to accept with being so financially advantaged?'

'I don't consider my finances an advantage,' she said seriously.

'Obviously, to have been earning a pittance working as a teacher.'

'How do you know what I earned?' she asked, lifting a brow.

'Do you think teachers' salaries are secret?'

She shook her head. 'It was more than enough to live on.'

At this, he regarded her through veiled eyes. 'So you chose not to access your vast trust fund?'

Feeling that there was more weight to the question than was obvious, she stuttered, 'W-why does that matter?'

'I'm curious as to why anyone would turn their back on a life of such privilege.'

She considered not answering him, but hadn't she been the one to insist they go into this marriage with the aim of making it work? And didn't that involve, at some point, opening the lines of communication? Besides, her feelings were no huge secret. 'I didn't want money to define me,' she said gently. 'I...found...people treat you differently when you're an heiress.' Her smile was grim. 'I didn't like that.'

His eyes roamed her face and she hated that he seemed to be reading her as one might a book. But after a moment he straightened, standing and holding a hand down to her. 'You experienced this when your mother died? And you went to live with your father?'

He wasn't touching her and yet his proximity was doing crazy things to her body. She was breathless and her tummy kept flopping, as though she'd crested over the high point of a rollercoaster. She nodded, not sure her voice wouldn't shake if she spoke.

'But money is just a part of who you are.'

She cleared her throat. 'The most important part, to many people.' Her lips twisted. 'Money, shares—even my marriage comes down to what I own, not who I am.'

At that he frowned, just an infinitesimal flicker of his lips, but he said nothing to dispute her summation. How could he? It was the truth.

'Do you feel up to finishing the tour?'

She sipped her water and nodded. 'Yes. I don't suppose you've had a map printed?' she said, only half joking. The place really was enormous.

'You'll get the hang of it,' he promised, holding a hand out to her. She put hers in his and he pulled her from the sofa. His fingers curled around hers and the pulse that had already been frantic went into overdrive. At this height, her gaze dropped to his lips and her mouth was dry as memories slammed into her from all angles.

'There are three bedrooms on this level,' he said, apparently oblivious to the tension that was zipping through Amelia. He gestured to their left as he guided her through the living space. Another step down and they were in yet another entertaining area, this time with a grand piano polished to a high sheen and panoramic views of the city in the distance. 'One can be for the nanny, and the other will be set up as a daytime nursery for the child.'

His words landed against her like little thuds. 'What nanny?'

He frowned. 'The child's nanny.' And at her darkening look he grimaced. 'There is no need to pull that cross face. I haven't hired anyone—you can do that. I'm simply saying this is where she will be accommodated. The third room along has its own kitchen and bathroom and is perfect for a live-in position.'

'Why in the world do you think I'd want to hire a nanny?'

He stopped walking, releasing her hand so he could thrust his hands into his pockets. 'Seriously?'

'Yes, seriously.' Her eyes narrowed. 'Did I ever say or do anything that implied I mightn't want to raise my child?'

'You *will* be raising him,' Antonio said with a frustration that belittled Amelia's feelings and caused anger to surge defensively through her, even when she knew she was possibly being a little over-sensitive. 'But you'll have help. Help for sleepless nights, help for long days, help with feeding or if the baby is restless or ill. Help, Amelia, is not the end of the world.'

'You sold me on this marriage by claiming you'd be a hands-on father and you're already trying to outsource the raising of a baby who hasn't even been born yet!'

He expelled a hiss of impatience. 'I am doing no such thing,' he said. 'A nanny just makes sense. When you go to work, who do you imagine will look after our child?'

'Work?' She blinked at him, the question so surprising it took her a moment to frame any kind of response.

'Yes, teaching. I presume you will want to return to work when our baby is older?'

'I…' A frown crossed her face. 'I thought you wouldn't want that.'

Now it was Antonio's turn to look confused. 'Why?'

Good question. 'Because you're…you. And I guess I thought you'd want me to be home with the baby, you know, being a mother…'

'You will still be a mother, I imagine,' he said, arching a single brow 'And I do not care if you work or not. My assumption was based on what I thought your preference would be. It's not a reflection of my wishes.'

'So you *don't* want me to work?'

'I just said I don't care either way,' he said with the appearance of patience. 'But if you are to return to work, we will need a solution to help, and I thought it would be better for the child if that person was someone they'd known from birth.'

It was all so damned logical and in her hormonal state that simply irritated her further. 'Where would I even work? I only speak Spanish curse words.'

At that he laughed and, ridiculously, she did too, and the tension that had been curling around them shivered a little and then gave way, like a dam bursting its banks. 'There is an international school,' he said quietly, 'just a few miles away. Lessons are conducted in English.'

'Teaching the children of rich moguls and tycoons?' she asked, still smiling.

'Teaching *children*,' he emphasised. 'Or are you so bigoted against wealth that you would judge the children who happen to be born to it?'

Another fair point that had her mood darkening once more. 'I'll think about it.'

'Fine,' he said. 'We have time to make a decision.'

Yes, that was true, time at least was on their side.

'The baby's room,' he said, opening the door to a room that currently housed little more than a bed and a small chest of drawers. 'Obviously we will have it decorated suitably once we know the gender.'

'I don't think I want to know what we're having. Not until it's born.'

'Why would you choose not to know?'

'I want the surprise,' she said with a shrug.

'You do not think the baby will be a surprise in and of itself?' he teased.

She tried to fight the temptation to banter with him. To succumb to his many, many charms. She'd done that once before and it had been disastrous.

'You're missing the point,' she said with an attempt at coldness.

'No, *querida.*' He shook his head. 'You are missing the point. We will decorate the room. We can paint it yellow. We can paint it green. We can paint it black, for all I care. We will make it a baby's room rather than this. Just as I do not care if you go back to work or not. I am showing you my house, and showing you how I think it can accommodate you and our family, and your future. I am trying to show you that I have thought this through, that I want this to work, just like you asked of me, yet you seem to want to argue with me at every turn. Why is that?'

She couldn't speak. Her heart was pounding, her mind was racing and her body was in flux. She was hot, despite the air-conditioning, and her cheeks felt flushed.

He took a step towards her, and then another, so that his strong body was almost touching hers. She stared up at him, her pale blue eyes meeting his stormy black ones and charging with electrical awareness. 'You are nervous,' he said simply.

'I'm not nervous,' she lied, her tongue darting out and licking her lower lip.

'You are nervous,' he said again. 'Because you are my wife, and I am your husband, and you do not know what that means. We married for a baby, but we never talked about this.'

'About what?' The words came out as a husky croak.

'About the fact that whatever madness drove us into bed that one time is still here, flaming at our feet.'

She drew in a sharp breath, surprise making her skin flush with goosebumps. 'No, it's not,' she said, raising her chin in a gesture of defiance that was completely belied by the way her eyes clung to his lips. 'Believe me, Antonio, I'm not so stupid that I'd make that mistake twice.'

His expression was scepticism itself. 'Really?'

'Really.' She nodded sharply. 'Sex has no part of this marriage.'

His smile was slow to unfurl and deadly in its danger to her. Because her heart began to beat off-rhythm and her pulse was thready. Legs that had been perfectly fine only minutes ago were wobbling now, threatening to give way.

'Do you realise how easily I could disprove that statement?'

She swallowed but it was useless, her mouth remained dry, as though coated with sawdust.

'Perhaps not,' he said, closing the distance between them. He didn't touch her, but oh, his body was so close she could feel his warmth through the fine fabric of her clothes and her body swayed forward of its own accord, so that her too sensitive nipples brushed against his chest and a soft, husky moan escaped her lips unbidden.

'You have no real experience,' he said, low and throaty. 'But what you're feeling now is desire.' He rocked his hips a fraction, so his arousal brushed against her and her eyes swept shut at his nearness and her needs.

'I'm feeling...' she said, searching for something, anything she could offer that would dispel his assertion. But nothing came to mind.

'Desire,' he supplied and then lifted a hand so he could smooth the ball of his thumb over her cheek.

'I don't...want you, like that,' she denied, so much more weakly than she would have liked. Her body—traitor that it was—pressed closer to his and when she blinked up at him her eyes were awash with desire and invitation.

His smile showed cynicism at her words, and then he stepped back. 'Yes, you do, *hermosa*, and I'm going to enjoy proving that to you.'

CHAPTER NINE

AMELIA FELT AS though she'd slept for three weeks and on a cloud. She awoke the next day completely relaxed, her body comfortable, her mind blank.

And then she looked around the room and it all came rushing back to her.

Holy heck, she was in Antonio's house. *Her* house. Their house! Because they were married!

The brief, but legally binding, ceremony came to her, and all that had taken place afterwards. She pushed out of bed, reaching for her phone—it sat on the bedside table. It was almost mid-morning!

She'd never slept so long in her entire life!

She was still wearing her wedding dress—if it could be called that. She'd worn it on the flight from England, and it wasn't even something she'd bought new for the event. She'd refused to observe any such kowtowing to tradition when their wedding was little more than a contractual agreement.

Yes, you do...and I'm going to enjoy proving that to you.

Awareness, hot and undeniable, pooled low in her abdomen. She galvanised her legs into action and made her way to the en-suite bathroom, where she freshened up. Her suitcase had been brought to this room at some point during her long rest. She cracked it open and pulled out a pair of shorts and a simple T-shirt, uncaring at how casual they were, refusing to feel the same insecurity when compared to Antonio's usual choice of lover.

Did it matter that the women he routinely slept with would probably swan about, draped in the latest couture dresses, all elegant and unapproachable, like this house?

Not to Amelia.

She wasn't going to let the ghosts of lovers past undermine her sense of self. With a nod to that commitment, she ventured out into the villa in search of Antonio.

Only the tour he'd given the day before, which had seemed to make perfect sense at the time, was a jumble in her mind. She found her way to the room he'd proposed using for the baby, and she saw it now with fresh, rested eyes and could admit it made perfect sense. In addition to being large, it was L-shaped, and she could imagine it with a small sofa and an armchair for nursing and, as he grew older, a little desk for his books and at which he could sit and do craft. It also lacked a terrace, and her concern for his safety made her glad for that.

The space beside the baby's room wasn't familiar to her. She pushed the door inwards and let out a gasp of surprise.

It was a library! A proper library. With thousands and thousands of books!

Antonio temporarily forgotten, she pushed deeper into the room, her breath unconsciously held as she scanned the spines. Many of the books were in Spanish; her heart dropped, but then it lifted once more.

So what? She had to learn the language—more than the bad words—at some point. Their son would be born in Spain, and his father was Spanish. In fact, their son or daughter would need to learn English, Spanish and Italian—all his heritages mixed together.

If they hired a nanny she would ensure it was someone bilingual, and perhaps she could include her own language tuition in the nanny's job description.

Only it was the second day of her marriage, she still knew barely anything about her husband—except that he was apparently more reasonable than she'd expected him to be—and she was most definitely getting ahead of herself.

She stepped out of the library and continued her walk through the house, heading downstairs and checking his office—empty—before moving to the ground floor.

A noise alerted her—splashing—and she went towards it.

It wasn't a particularly surprising discovery that he should be in the pool, but when she stepped onto the timber deck she stopped walking abruptly and could only stare.

Antonio was doing laps, and he wore only a skimpy pair of black briefs. As his legs kicked and his arms pulled him through the water, she stared at him, her eyes chasing his movements, her body hot all over.

He turned underwater and when he came up for breath, midway through another length, his eyes met hers and he stopped, standing in the pool water. The look he sent her was a more powerful aphrodisiac than even the image of him pulling through the water.

It was a look of absolute speculation, and something more. Something else altogether, like fierce masculine possession. Her fingers knotted in front of her, echoing the knots in her stomach. 'I thought I was going to have to wake you,' he said after a moment. 'It is almost midday.'

She nodded, moving closer to the pool and dipping her toe in. The water was delightfully cool. 'I know. I can't believe it. I guess that's pregnancy.'

He was watchful, his intelligent eyes moving analytically over her face. 'The books I read all say exhaustion is a symptom.'

'You've read pregnancy books?'

He frowned then shrugged, so water droplets ran over his shoulders and her eyes dropped to his smooth caramel flesh. 'Of course.'

He swam across the pool, coming to the coping right beside Amelia's feet. 'Have there been any other symptoms?' he asked, looking directly up at her.

She sat down, dropping her legs into the water and kicking them forward. The relief was heaven against her warm skin. 'A bit of nausea.' She shrugged. 'A headache, from time to time. Nothing remarkable.'

'How did you discover you were pregnant?'

'I went to the doctor,' she said simply.

'But why? Were you ill?'

'Oh, no. I just…the dates.' She shook her head, remembering that surreal moment. 'I couldn't believe it.'

'Did you think about keeping it from me?'

She looked away from him, swallowing. 'Not for even a second,' she said honestly.

She didn't see the way his lips pulled downwards at the corner. 'That surprises me.'

'Why?'

'You hardly know me, as you pointed out. And our family situation…'

She shook her head. 'I think what's surprising is that any woman would keep a baby from its father. A child isn't solely a mother's or a father's. To deprive someone of being a parent, for whatever reason…it seems wrong.'

'I agree,' he said, steel in the words. 'From the moment you told me I was a father my world changed. I cannot imagine how I would feel if you had elected to keep this to yourself.'

She swallowed past a lump in her throat as memories of her own childhood taunted her. 'To raise our baby to think either that their father didn't want them, or wondering at who and why… I wouldn't do that.'

Perhaps the words were laced with her own pain because, beneath the water, one of his hands wrapped gently around her ankle and he stroked it, so that heat flared in her skin. 'You weren't close to your own father, growing up.'

They both knew the truth of that statement.

But Amelia sighed heavily, regarding him with eyes that were unknowingly wary. 'No.' She bit down on her lip and focused on the small patterns formed in the water's reflection. 'I didn't even know who he was until my mother died.'

'You mean you'd never met him?' he enquired with obvious disbelief, moving to stand in front of her now, transferring his grip so he had a hand clamped around each of her ankles.

'I mean I'd never met him, and I didn't even know his name.' Her eyes dropped to the water. 'My mother never told me about him.'

'But he knew of you?'

'No.'

'*No?*' The word was bitten out with shock.

'No. She never told him about me. And any time I asked her about my father she'd get angry, and then say she couldn't remember, as though falling pregnant was something trivial and unimportant.'

Her face flashed with emotion. 'When she died her lawyer gave me the answers I'd wanted all my life—and, because I was a minor, I was sent to live with my father—a man who was as blindsided by my existence as I was his.'

A muscle jerked in his square jaw and her gaze fell to it instinctively. 'How could she have been so selfish?'

'That was my mother,' Amelia observed drily. 'She was the absolute definition of selfish. I suppose she thought she'd never die—utterly juvenile, given her lifestyle. Or maybe she thought she'd tell me when I was older. More likely, she just didn't think it through at all. She definitely knew who my father was, though, because in her will—and, believe me, I was shocked to discover she'd had the maturity to even draft one—my parentage was clearly noted. To this day, I have no idea why she chose to raise me on her own. God knows there were about a thousand things she'd have preferred to do with her life.'

The pain-filled invective lay around them, dark and spiky. Antonio's fingers stroked the flesh at her ankles and he stood at her legs, looking up at her contemplatively. 'And did your father take you in straight away?'

Her cheeks stained pink as the mortification of that summer wrapped around her anew. 'You make me sound like a puppy,' she said with a shake of her head, in an attempt to lighten the conversation.

He didn't smile. 'Did he?'

'More or less,' she answered, her eyes sparking with memories. 'He had a DNA test to be sure. I can't blame him,' Amelia was quick to offer in defence. 'Their relationship was brief, and he never heard from my mother again. His scepticism makes sense.'

'Perhaps. But I imagine his caution hurt you, as a young woman?'

Her expression was wary. 'I understood,' she said sharply, unable to admit the deep pain she'd felt at his decision.

'And once the results came back?'

Now her smile was brittle. 'I was a diSalvo, beyond a shadow of doubt,' she said. 'He laid proud claim to me in much the same manner you are to our baby. That's the way it works in dynasties like this, isn't it? Children are heirs more than they are people.'

Antonio's face was a mask of careful consideration. 'I think children are both.'

Amelia shifted her gaze away from his. 'Perhaps. In any event, I was no longer a child.'

'You were twelve?'

Twelve—still so young, she realised now. 'Nearly thirteen. And I'd been living with my mum so I'd seen a lot.'

Her smile was a rejection, a way of shutting the conversation down. 'It's all water under the bridge now.'

It was unusual for Antonio to have a conversation shift away from him, even more unusual to have it purposely pulled. He didn't want to allow the change in direction. There was too much he wanted to know.

But it was the first day of their marriage—an interrogation could wait, surely? He had all the time in the world to find the answers he wanted.

So he smiled calmly and then scooped some water up and flicked it at her. Her surprise was obvious and he wondered how she'd react, watching her, waiting.

Then she laughed, and returned volley, reaching down and lashing him with a heavy spray of pool water before reaching down once more. This time he caught her wrist and pulled, so she fell into the pool with him. She went underwater, then bounced back to the surface, dashing her hair away from her eyes.

She blinked, clearing her eyes, and the air between them seemed to charge. Her breasts were clearly visible beneath the saturated cotton of her T-shirt, bobbing on the water and, out of nowhere, he remembered the way they'd felt in his palms, the way he'd taken her nipples into his mouth, and his body was tight and hard beneath the water.

'Race you to the other side,' she challenged and, before he could answer, she was off. He watched her stroke for several seconds before powering to catch up with her. Yes, an interrogation would wait—there were better ways to spend the first day of their marriage.

Dinner was a surprisingly easy affair. Antonio was a skilled conversationalist and he kept things light, enquiring about her time at university and her job at Hedgecliff Academy.

It was no hardship for her to talk about her pupils and her work, the school she'd come to love.

What she didn't say was the part it had played in her recovery—she'd lost her mother and she'd chosen to turn her back on her father and her brother. Oh, there was no scandal, no unpleasant estrangement, but she'd walked away from them and all they stood for, choosing to live the life she'd always fantasised about.

A quiet life, with simple pleasures and easy friendships.

She didn't say how Hedgecliff had pulled her back together when she'd been searching for her real identity, separating herself from the girl who'd been the daughter of a supermodel and then a billion-pound heiress.

And whether he had questions or not, she didn't know because he moved their talk along, sharing his own stories of his time at university—his degree at Cambridge, and then he'd done postgraduate study at Harvard, which explained why his English was so perfect. And all the while he'd been overseeing his family business.

She knew from previous conversations that these years would have involved a time when Giacomo and Carlo were actively trying to ruin Herrera Incorporated, but he glossed over that too, undoubtedly for her benefit.

It was a pleasant night, and if Amelia had been asked two weeks earlier if that was possible she would have sworn until she was blue in the face that there was nothing on earth that would induce her to spend a nice quiet evening with Antonio Herrera—and especially not to enjoy it.

But dinner drew to a close and the sun dipped low over Madrid, setting late in the evening owing to the time of year. They were just two people then, with night before them, and all she could think about was the way he'd looked at her earlier.

She'd said she didn't want him, and he'd contradicted that.

Yes, you do, hermosa, *and I'm going to enjoy proving that to you.*

'Well,' she said, awkwardness in the small word, 'I might go to bed.'

She couldn't quite meet his eyes.

He didn't respond directly. 'Have you told your family about this?'

She was very still, her heart heavy inside her. 'Not yet.'

At that, she felt him stiffen. 'You haven't mentioned our marriage?'

'Nope.'

'Your pregnancy?'

She shook her head from side to side.

'*Dios mío!* For what reason?'

She chewed on her lower lip, reaching for her water glass and sipping from it to bring some moistness back to her dry mouth. 'It's complicated,' she said after a moment.

'Complicated? To tell them you are pregnant?' He stood, and her eyes dragged up his frame, drawn to his strength and breadth as though he were a magnet.

'You're not just some man to them, though. You're the devil, remember?' Her brows knit together. 'The fact I'm in some kind of relationship with you would be enough to kill them,' she muttered. 'Let alone when they realise it was just a stupid one-night stand from which I ended up pregnant.'

His expression was inscrutable as he came to crouch beside her, his trousers stretched over his powerful haunches.

'Come on,' she said with a roll of her eyes. 'You hate them; obviously they feel the same about you. And the last thing I want is for me or my baby to become some kind of pawn in your feud. If they knew I was pregnant, they'd have absolutely refused to let me marry you.'

He arched his brows and reached a hand for her chin, holding her face still when she would have turned away from him. 'And you'd have let them control your life in that way?'

'No.' Her eyes sparked with his. 'Because I'm doing this for the baby, because I want him or her to have a family, remember?' She sighed. 'I didn't want them trying to stop the wedding, and I didn't want them making a huge deal out of this.'

He frowned. 'It's ironic that you are attempting to keep our marriage a secret,' he said with a grimace.

'Why is that ironic? Can't you see that it makes sense?'

'No,' he said firmly, with a shake of his head.

'I obviously plan on telling them some time. I just... don't quite know when,' she finished vaguely.

In truth, the idea of having that conversation sat heavily on her shoulders. Nothing about this pregnancy was straightforward. Not the circumstances, not the baby's father, and certainly not the family history that shrouded their child, even before birth. And yet, in spite of that, one emotion had overridden all others: happiness. And, selfishly, she didn't want anything to detract from that. Giacomo and Carlo would be furious—and she understood why. But she didn't want to have that discussion yet. There was enough to adapt to—marriage to Antonio, getting to know him, settling into life in Madrid, dealing with her pregnancy.

Her family would have questions, and she'd feel better answering them when she knew exactly what those answers were! To have to defend her marriage, to explain her reasoning, to permit intrusions into what was a private matter—she didn't want that. She wasn't ready for it.

'Then you will not wish them to join us.'

'Join us?' She stared at him with alarm. 'What for?'

He dropped his hand away from her face. 'I've arranged a small wedding reception to take place next week. My friends and business associates, nothing big, but I thought you should meet them, and that they should meet you. I had wondered if you'd like your family to be there too. I must say, I'm relieved this is not the case.'

Amelia's heart began to race in her chest. Ignoring any suggestion of her father and brother coming face to face with the father of her child, a man they already hated, she focused on the rest of his statement. 'A party?'

'A cocktail party,' he agreed, making it sound civilised when she knew what these things were like. God, she'd been to more than her fair share, first with her mother and then courtesy of her second life as a diSalvo. 'Some music, food, champagne, fifty or so people. It will be over within a few hours but, vitally, it will cement our marriage.'

'Cement our marriage?' She scraped her chair back, standing with a sense of panic. 'I thought the document we signed did that. You know, the ceremony in front of a judge, the fact our marriage has been registered with the Spanish court?'

'I mean socially.'

'Socially? You actually care about that?'

He reached for the plates, carrying them through to the kitchen. She followed out of curiosity.

'I care about your life here in Madrid,' he surprised her by saying, stacking the dishwasher then turning to face her. 'I don't want you to be lonely and, the truth is, I work long hours. I thought you'd like to make some friends—there'll be women at the party, friends of mine. You'll like them.'

She gasped in a hot, angry breath and pushed away any thought that his gesture was one of kindness. 'You're actually trying to make my friendships for me? You really do have the most insufferable God complex.'

'And you have the ability to twist any gesture into some kind of insult,' he volleyed back, crossing his arms over his chest. She refused to analyse his words, nor to see truth in them. 'What did you think marriage to me would entail? Did you presume we would have no social life whatsoever?'

'I…presumed you'd go about your business as always and I'd be free to do my own thing.'

His eyes sparked with dark emotions. 'You believed wrong. You are my wife. You could do me the courtesy of at least trying to act like it, so far as the world is concerned.'

Her jaw dropped at this demand, so too did her heart speed up at his blatant claim of possession. *You are my wife.* How those words trickled down her spine like warmed honey, filling her with pleasure and pain all at once.

'But this isn't a real marriage,' she said weakly, when other words and pleas were swarming through her mind.

'You want to bet?' he volleyed back, and now his hands were braced on either side of her body, his palms pressed into the bench, his frame a perfect jail for her. She stared up at him, helpless and lost, and there was a threat in his eyes that filled her with desire.

'I…'

'You what?' he asked, dropping his head so his face hovered only an inch above hers.

'I…'

'Yes, *querida*?' he demanded, lowering his face still, so his lips brushed hers and a jolt of electricity fired up her spine. 'Tell me again how this marriage of ours is not a real one.' And his lips did more than buzz against hers then, they pressed to her mouth and she whimpered, low in her throat. Her fingers, of their own volition, grasped the sides of his shirt and he deepened the kiss when her lips parted on another moan. His tongue slid into her mouth and then he lifted her as though she weighed nothing, sitting her on the benchtop so he could stand between her legs and plunder her mouth as if he was the only man on earth.

And, God, wasn't he? For her at least?

But she'd fallen prey to this desire once before. It had flashed into her life and she'd been weak—too weak to realise that he could use this sensuality like a drug. She couldn't submit to it again—it would be foolish.

His fingers found the bottom of her shirt and he lifted it just enough for his fingertips to graze her bare flesh and every cell in her body cried out in relief and delight, and hope. Hope that he would strip her naked and make love to her once more.

With a guttural, desperate cry, she pulled away from him, moving back on the bench and lifting her fingers to her lips, lips that were bruised and throbbing with desire.

'How dare you?' The words were strangled from deep within her, and they were saturated with self-recrimination because she had wanted him to kiss her. She hadn't wanted him to stop kissing her!

He narrowed his eyes, and they were as clouded by desire as her own. 'How dare I what? Kiss you as you have been wanting me to all night? Kiss you as though you are my wife?'

'I haven't,' she denied hotly, but it was a lie and they both knew that.

He spoke without responding to her denial, but his voice was husky, filled with the passion that had flamed between them just now. 'How *dare* I want you to have friends? To have a social life here in Madrid? People to catch up with when I am travelling for work? Other mothers to talk to about babies and nappies and bottles and I don't know what else?'

She was glad to return to their argument, rather than have to defend the way she'd melted in his arms. 'That's up to me!' she snapped from teeth that were clamped together. 'I'm perfectly capable of making my own friends.'

'But you don't want them to be my friends,' he surmised, his expression shifting.

'I didn't say that.' She bit down on her lip, trying to find words that would defuse this, that would explain her hesitation. 'This has all happened so fast. I just need a moment to catch my breath before I start thinking about everything else.'

'It is a party. My friends, some food, music, dancing. You will enjoy yourself.'

It was the wrong thing to say. Panic filled her mouth with a taste of adrenalin. Everything was happening too fast. 'I can't do that.' She thought of all the parties she'd been to—first with her mother, then as a diSalvo heiress, and a shiver scratched over her spine.

'I'm sure it seems inconsequential to you, but it's not to me. It's too much, too fast.' She shook her head. 'No party. Please.'

His eyes narrowed and she was reminded that one of the many facets of this man was the ruthless, hard-nosed tycoon. That he conquered whatever he turned his hand to in the corporate world. That he was determined and he was fierce and that he was used to getting his own way.

'When you agreed to marry me, you told me you wanted me to be reasonable. Is there anything unreasonable about what I'm proposing?'

'Yes!' she snapped, and then shook her head because there wasn't.

'What is it, Amelia? Do you think you can keep this marriage secret for ever?'

'I...' She shook her head. 'This is not negotiable.' The words trembled with the strength of her emotion.

He exhaled softly and his warm breath fanned her temple, so her body swayed forward infinitesimally of its own accord. 'You're saying you wish me to cancel it?'

'Yes,' she responded quickly, too quickly, as her throat constricted. Her breath was hard and fast. How could she explain to him what her life had been like? At least, with Penny, Amelia had been dragged to events with an eclectic, artsy crowd. With the diSalvos it had been designer chic the whole way. Designer drugs, designer cars, designer everything. Amelia had never belonged, hadn't wanted to belong, and she'd fled that scene as soon as she could. The thought of being right back in the midst of it was impossible to countenance.

'Fine,' he said darkly, his disapproval obvious. 'Consider it cancelled. Now, if you'll excuse me, I have work to do.'

CHAPTER TEN

ANTONIO STARED AT the document and reread the contents for the tenth time in as many minutes. It was a simple feasibility study, the kind of thing he usually ate for breakfast, but on this night his mind simply wouldn't focus.

His eyes drifted to the clock above his desk: it was into the small hours of the morning and he was still seething over their argument. Over her intractability, yes, but also over his own actions. And something else niggled at the back of his mind—the way her eyes had flooded with emotions he couldn't quite unravel. It had made him want, more than anything, to understand her.

He'd organised the party out of a desire to smooth her transition into his life. Where the hell had that concern come from?

Why had he bothered?

True, she was pregnant with his baby, but had that fact completely erased all others? She was a diSalvo, and their family rivalry wasn't likely to be forgotten easily. Not with a party, not with a baby, not with anything.

His attempts to pretend otherwise were futile. He was better to focus on what they had, and what they were, and forget anything else.

She was a beautiful woman and their chemistry was off the charts. If she chose to join him in bed, then so be it. He wasn't going to lose sleep over her choice there. Their kiss, though, forced its way into his consciousness and his arousal strained against his jeans. She had wanted him then, and he had wanted her. Pleasure had been within reach. Only she'd pushed him away, as though the heat that flamed between them wasn't going to demand an answer at some point.

And it would: the call of their bodies was too strong to resist. But he would bide his time and let the desire between them swamp her, drive her to the point of madness, and then he would be there, when she was so desperate for his touch that she couldn't think straight.

And in the meantime nothing would be allowed to derail his reasons for marrying her. He wanted Prim'Aqua. He wanted the men who'd hurt his father to pay—and his marriage would bring that about, one way or another.

He kicked back in his chair, his fingers interlocking behind his head as he closed his eyes.

And saw Amelia, her huge blue eyes accusing in her face, her lips pulled downwards, a look of bewilderment on her expression.

She'd hate him, but he'd cross that bridge when he came to it.

Nothing could be allowed to alter his course. Nothing, and no one…not even the woman who was carrying his baby. She'd made it obvious she didn't welcome his involvement in her life, and didn't want his help. *So let her be,* he told himself. *Let her find her feet, have her breathing room and space.*

What the hell did he care?

Three weeks into their marriage and Amelia would have given her left arm for some civil conversation. It wasn't exactly that her husband *was* uncivil, he was perfectly polite, but the easy rapport they'd established on that first day had completely evaporated. So too the sexual tension that had threatened to unzip her completely.

They hadn't shared a meal together either. He'd made

a point of explaining his absences—he was working on a big deal and needed to be in his office late. It made sense for her to eat without him, he'd explained, giving her the number for the woman who prepared his meals so she could order whatever she wanted.

But three weeks into their marriage and she knew she had to speak to him. She'd tried to organise things herself but, with her limited language and no car at her disposal, she was hampered in a way she found utterly frustrating.

He worked late into the evening, not returning to the house until almost eleven o'clock. But, unlike previous nights, when she'd been in her own room, either fast asleep or pretending to be, Amelia was awake when he returned, dressed, sipping a cup of chamomile tea.

He clearly wasn't expecting it, if the look on his face was anything to go by. And he looked...tired. She only had a moment to glimpse that before he flattened his face of any emotion and looked at her with mild curiosity. As though she were a creature who'd wandered into his home, a unicorn or narwhal, utterly mystical and somewhat novel.

'Amelia? I thought you'd be asleep.'

'I need to speak with you,' she said softly, then cleared her throat. Her body screamed at his closeness, her lips throbbed and a drum began to beat low down in her abdomen, demanding attention.

'Oh?' He moved deeper into the sitting area, placing a document wallet down on the front hallstand. 'Is there a problem?'

'No.' She shook her head. 'Not really.'

'Good.' He expelled a breath, a sound which might have been one of relief or impatience. But she ignored it. This was important.

'I need your help.'

That had his attention. His eyes narrowed and he strode closer. 'You are sure everything is okay? The baby...?'

'The baby's fine, so far as I know.'

'What do you mean?'

'I'm twelve weeks into the pregnancy,' she said. 'I remember the doctor I saw in England telling me I'd need a scan around now. And some other tests. Only I don't speak Spanish and I have no idea where to go. I've tried to use online translation to find somewhere but it's pretty impossible, to be honest. And anyway I don't have a car here, though I guess I could get a taxi—but where would I get a taxi *to*?'

He stared at her, his expression shifting from confusion to something else, an anger that was self-inflicted. 'Of course,' he said, and his frown deepened. 'I'm sorry to say that hadn't occurred to me.'

'Why would it?' she asked shyly. 'It's not like you've had a baby before. This is all new to both of us.'

He frowned. 'Still, it's not exactly rocket science.'

'The doctor in England referred me to a clinic in London. Obviously that's not much good here.'

He turned away from her, striding towards the panoramic windows. His hands were on his hips and his back moved with the increased pace of his breathing.

'I have many cars. You are welcome to drive any of them.'

She frowned, following the thread of conversation. His cars were all fast, expensive, sleek and powerful. She shook her head gently. 'I'd prefer to buy something myself, something that's not got the horsepower of a wild beast beneath the bonnet. Except I don't even know where to do that.'

He turned to face her, his expression grim. 'Fine. We'll buy you a new car.'

'I can buy myself a new car,' she chided softly. 'I just need your help to…do that.'

'Fine.' Frustration zapped in the air between them, like lightning hitting a river.

'Thank you.' She cleared her throat and tried to break the silence with a smile. It felt strange on her lips—she hadn't smiled in a long time. Not since leaving England?

His eyes flashed in warning. 'Don't thank me for this, Amelia. I should have thought of it. I am truly sorry I overlooked all these practicalities—it's not like me to overlook anything. You must have felt like my prisoner here, after all.'

'It's fine. I've been reading, and swimming, and...' Her words petered out as he took a step closer, and then her breath grew heavy and her eyes swept shut.

'It is *not* fine,' he said simply, his accent thick. 'Please accept my apology.'

What she would have preferred was an apology for his absence.

'Fine, apology accepted,' she agreed unevenly. 'Now, about the appointment. I've been searching online and I *think* I've found a good obstetrics clinic.' She held her phone out to him and he took it, but his eyes remained locked to hers.

The air between them was charged and yet she was powerless to look away. Her eyes were held to his by an invisible magnetism, too strong to ignore. 'I just can't read the reviews,' she said, the words husky.

He held her phone but didn't look at it. 'How are you feeling?' The question was husky, drawn from the depths of his soul.

She blinked, but didn't shift her gaze.

'I...' Of their own accord, her hands lifted to her stomach and, as always, her heart lifted at the thought of the life that was growing there. 'Good.'

Now their eyes parted as his moved briefly to her gesture, and then his free hand was lifting like hers, moving over her stomach slowly.

Surprise was in his eyes, surprise and wonderment. He

curved his palm over the very faint hint of roundness, and when he spoke it was with a voice thickened by emotion. 'Are you well?'

Inexplicable tears formed in Amelia's eyes. She tried to blink them back, but one escaped unbidden and slid down her cheek.

Irritated by it, she grimaced. It was just that she'd been so lonely, and seeing him now, feeling him touch her stomach and feel the life that was growing there—how could she not be affected?

'I'm fine.' The words were slightly uneven.

He nodded slowly, then dropped his hand and, finally, the spell was broken. He turned to her phone, scanning the page she'd shown him, and nodding curtly. 'It looks fine. I will make enquiries in the morning and organise an appointment.'

'Thank you.' She turned on her heel, ready to leave the room, her brain unable to supply anything else to say.

But he forestalled her with a softly voiced, 'Would you like something to drink? A cup of tea?'

Her eyes swept shut and she was glad she had her back to him, so that he wouldn't see the complex knot of emotions that passed over her face.

'I haven't eaten,' he said. 'Join me.'

It was a simple invitation, spontaneously given, but it set off a cascade effect in Amelia. She'd missed him. Not him, *per se,* so much as a person to speak to, and laugh with. Or maybe it was all him—Antonio Herrera, the man who seemed to breathe life into her dreams and torment her sleeping body with memories of his touch.

Temptation was the devil and she knew she needed to fight it. To fight the desire to lean into him and ask him to hold her tight, to have him smile at her as he had that first night—even if she knew it would be a lie.

'I'm tired,' she said, turning to face him for a brief moment, heat warming her body, memories making her ache for the past. 'I… I think I'll just go to bed.'

She *had* looked tired, he admitted to himself, staring out at the shimmering surface of the pool, Scotch cradled in the palm of his hand. The moon was high overhead, casting a silver light over the water.

He'd spent the last three weeks holed up in his office, working late, yes, but also actively avoiding his wife.

Avoiding her enormous blue eyes that showed him the galaxy, avoiding the softness of her body, the addictive properties of her smile. He'd been avoiding her and tonight he fully understood why.

One look at her and he knew he'd run in front of a freight train to protect her and the baby that was growing inside her. One word from her and he was at risk of turning his back on everything he'd worked towards.

One word and he could almost genuinely forget his hatred for her family. It wasn't personal. It had nothing to do with Amelia. It was the baby; that was all. Some ancient, ingrained primal instinct was firing inside him, demanding he fulfil his duty and keep her and the baby safe and well. Even if that made him willing to surrender his own needs.

Weakness was foreign to him, and it sure as hell wasn't welcome. She wore his ring; she carried his baby, but she was still a diSalvo—and he couldn't forget that.

He shut his eyes and tried not to think of his wife. He forced his mind to erase her image momentarily, and replace it with the image of his father. He brought to mind painful memories that he generally chose to disregard, memories of his father's stress and grief and the first time Antonio had confronted Carlo with what he'd done, and Carlo had laughed in Antonio's face. Carlo had made an enemy that day—and Antonio knew he'd never be able to forget that.

Forgiveness might have been divine, but it was nowhere on Antonio's radar.

'Seriously, though, was the helicopter really necessary?' Amelia asked as the chief of the obstetrics wing of the Hospital Internacional de Madrid exited the exam room for a moment.

The room was dark, the lights off, a heavy blackout curtain blotting out all of Spain's sunshine. Medical devices surrounded them, casting a very soft glow—one that was almost eerie.

He tilted her a sardonic glance. 'Of course. I wanted to see how long it would take to get here in an emergency.'

And, despite the fact she'd told herself she would remain distant from him, she found herself rolling her eyes teasingly. 'A car would suffice.'

'You never know,' he said, and he was serious now, his eyes showing a strength that made her tummy flip and flop.

'Mr and Mrs Herrera.' Dr López returned, a kindly smile on his face. He must have been in his sixties, with steel-grey hair and a lined face, and his experience gave Amelia confidence. 'I have this,' he said, holding up a bottle. 'It will feel cold at first, okay?'

Amelia nodded, lying back on the narrow bed.

Dr López pushed Amelia's shirt up, right to the ridge of her bra, and he wiggled the waistband of her skirt lower, exposing her gently rounded stomach. The gel he applied was ice-cold but it wasn't unpleasant, given the heat and humidity of the day.

Once he'd finished, he smiled reassuringly and moved to the other side of the bed. 'Let us take a look.'

Amelia was inexplicably nervous and, almost as though he understood that, Antonio reached out and curved his hand over hers, squeezing her fingers in his. She blinked up at him and a throb of strong emotion passed between them. She wrenched her gaze away, hating that her hormones made her so close to tears at present.

Dr López pressed the ultrasound wand to her belly, firmly enough that she was slightly uncomfortable, and now she squeezed Antonio's hand.

'Okay?' he asked huskily.

'Yeah,' she whispered.

'The baby is playing hide and seek,' the doctor reassured them both. 'Just a minute.'

Amelia held her breath, waiting—tense, nervous, anxious, delirious with every emotion she could imagine.

'And you have not been unwell?' Dr López asked, his expression infuriatingly blank.

Amelia swallowed. 'No. I mean, I've been a little sick sometimes.'

'Good.' He nodded, and Amelia relaxed. Beside her, though, she was aware of tension emanating from Antonio that caused her heart to twist in her chest.

'You can see here your baby—' Dr López pointed to the screen '—lying on its back, see?'

'Whoa…' Amelia blinked, tears filling her eyes now, and Antonio squeezed her hand tight '…that's our baby.' She blinked up at her husband and the sight of him, still as a rock, his own eyes suspiciously moist, made everything hurt.

'Yes, looking quite happy, you'd have to say.'

Their baby was still so tiny, just a blip on the screen, but already her heart was bursting with love and total vulnerability.

'You will need to come back in a month or so,' Dr López said, pushing the screen away and handing Amelia a soft towel. She wiped her stomach clean of gel and then placed a hand over her belly.

'And this is my card, with my personal number,' he addressed Antonio.

Her husband took the card with a curt nod. No gratitude, nothing to express that the chief of the hospital giving his private number to a patient was anything unusual. Because he was used to that kind of treatment. Doors opened for Antonio. He got what he wanted, when he wanted it.

'If you have any concerns at any time, you may call,' Dr Lopez continued. 'Otherwise, I'll see you in another month.'

He pulled some small square pieces of paper from beneath the screen and handed them to Amelia. Fresh tears welled in her eyes as she stared at the grainy first photographs of her baby.

And then, slowly, she looked at Antonio and bit down on her lip. Because, whatever doubts she'd had about this marriage, whatever had come before, in that moment—she had none. No doubts, no reservations, no regrets. She reached for his hand and squeezed it, her smile brighter than a thousand suns.

'Can you believe it?'

He shook his head slowly. 'Not even for a moment.' He rubbed his thumb over the back of her hand and then leaned down, pressing a kiss to her cheek, so close to the corner of her lips that a small nudge of her face in that direction would have connected lips to lips. But she stayed still, her eyes blinking closed as she breathed him in.

'Shall we go for lunch, Mrs Herrera?'

Right on cue, her stomach gave a low grumble and she nodded slowly. 'That sounds like a fine idea.'

Just a little way from the Parque del Retiro, down a small side street with brightly coloured buildings on either side, lined with large trees and small colourful shrubs, was a restaurant so exclusive there was no visible name. Just a black door—easily missed unless you knew where you were going—showed the entrance.

Antonio pressed a hand in the small of Amelia's back, the touch purely civil—it was a gesture that wouldn't have been out of place between colleagues, yet it was like a match being sparked low in her abdomen, and tiny flames burned in every single nerve ending. He pressed a button and a minute later a waiter appeared, wearing jeans and a white shirt, with a butcher's apron tied around his waist. He addressed them in rapid-fire Spanish, so Antonio responded in English.

'For two, on the terrace.'

'Immediately,' the waiter said, switching effortlessly to Amelia's native language.

The small door opened into a huge room, so light and airy it was like being in the countryside. Windows that should have looked out onto the street had been screened with green, creating the illusion of being in a garden paradise, and the ceilings were at least three storeys high.

There was a lift at the back and the waiter pressed a button, waiting beside them for it to arrive. Once the doors had opened, he held the doors then reached inside to press a button, before nodding and spinning on his heel.

The lift ascended swiftly—it took only seconds—and then they were on a terrace that exceeded all of Amelia's expectations. It overlooked the park, showing verdant rolling hills in one direction, and large trees grew in huge pots, jasmine scrambled over a pergola and the tables were placed haphazardly—scattered at random, so that no one table was near another.

It was perfect—private, intimate and clearly exclusive without being off-putting.

'Ah, Mr Herrera.' Another waiter appeared, this one a little older, with his dark hair thinning at the temples, his eyes holding Antonio's before transferring to Amelia. 'Lovely of you to join us again.'

Amelia ignored the instant surge of jealousy at that—because of course Antonio had frequented this restaurant before, and presumably not alone. It was the perfect place to bring a date—hadn't she just been thinking so? She straightened her spine, telling herself she didn't—couldn't, shouldn't—care.

'This way, please.' The waiter smiled at Amelia and then guided them to a table right at the edge of the terrace. Here, the fragrance of jasmine was exquisite and a nearby citrus tree in a pot was in blossom, so there was a faint humming of feeding bees, their pollen collectors glistening yellow in the afternoon light. The sun was high in the sky yet it wasn't unbearably warm. Amelia took the seat Antonio had held out for her, letting her gaze chase the details of the view.

For the first time, she felt a kernel of excitement for this—her new city. There was so much to explore, so much to learn!

'It's beautiful,' she said after a moment, her breath fast.

He looked towards the park, and pushed his sunglasses up onto his head. She transferred her attention from the park to Antonio, marvelling at how easy it was to forget just how intensely attractive he was.

'Yes.' He ran a hand over his stubbled chin. 'When I was a boy,' he said, turning to look at her and smiling an easy, companionable smile, 'my father used to take me there, almost every weekend.'

'Really? What for?'

'Football,' he said with a shrug so his shirt drew across his shoulders and she bit down on her lip to remind herself not to stare. 'And puppets.'

'Puppets?'

A waiter appeared with some sparkling water, placing it on the table before them.

'Puppets,' Antonio agreed, once they were alone again. 'There are puppet shows on, all the time, and I used to love them.'

Her heart turned over in her chest at this unexpected detail from his childhood—so mundane, so regular, and completely perfect.

'You're surprised?' he prompted, despite the fact she'd said nothing—and she knew it was because he could read her more easily with each day that passed.

'I'm...yes,' she said on a curt nod. 'I am.'

'Why?'

'Because you don't strike me as a man who was ever really a boy,' she said, and then wrinkled her nose on a small laugh, which he echoed.

'You think I was born like this?'

'No.' She rolled her eyes, her smile not fading. 'I guess you must have physically been a boy at some point. But one that played and had fun?'

He wiggled his brows. 'I assure you, I was both those things.'

'You weren't determined to take over the world, even at six?'

'Perhaps a little,' he said, lifting his hand, his forefinger and thumb pressed close together.

The waiter returned, brandishing menus, and Antonio took them without looking in the waiter's direction.

'Thank you,' Amelia murmured, flying the flag of civility for both of them.

'And you?' Antonio pushed, after the waiter had left. 'Was your childhood full of fun?'

Amelia bristled. 'I'm sure you know the answer to that.' She reached for her water, sipping it, turning back to the view. Inexplicably, her heart was racing.

'I have an impression,' he agreed with an air of relaxation. 'But you have not told me specifics.'

'With good reason.' She tilted a small smile at him. 'I don't like to speak about it.'

Speculation glowed in the depths of his eyes, eyes that were—at times—dark black, and now showed specks of amber and caramel. 'Then make an exception on this occasion. For me.'

CHAPTER ELEVEN

HE WATCHED AS she considered those words, wondering at the sense of reserve she wore like a cloak. It hadn't been there on the night in her cottage, when she'd brandished a meat cleaver and made him laugh, despite the seriousness of his business with the diSalvo family. Was it him that unsettled her?

The nature of their marriage?

Inwardly he cringed—how could it be anything else? Blackmailing someone into marriage was hardly a way to encourage closeness. Yet here they sat, husband and wife—as much an enigma to one another as the day they'd first met.

'I think,' she said, and he didn't realise until then that he'd been holding his breath, waiting for her to speak and half believing she wouldn't, 'some people would characterise it as fun.' She wrinkled her nose and his gut twisted, hard. He made an effort not to move, to appear natural, but it was as though he was hyper aware of every movement he made, every movement she made.

'But not you?' he asked, the words low and husky.

'No.' Her eyes met his and there was that thread of defiance, a whip of strength, that made his body arc up in immediate response. 'Not me.' She smiled, a tight smile, as she reached for her water glass, sipping from it slowly, her eyes landing on the view beyond them. 'I think the novelty of freedom is exactly that—a novelty. As a child I was always afraid.' She cleared her throat, and said no more.

So he prompted, 'Afraid of what?'

'What my mother would do.'

As though screws were being turned in every joint, his body tightened. 'She hurt you?'

'Oh, God, no.' She spun back toward him, her eyes enormous, and he could see so much of the famed supermodel in his wife's face that he wondered if they were alike in ways other than the physical. 'My mother was the kindest person you could ever meet. *Too* kind.'

'Is there such a thing?'

Amelia's frown was instantaneous but it was as though a storm cloud was moving in front of the sun. 'Modelling is a hard business. You can never be the prettiest, the skinniest, the best. She spent her life trying.' Amelia shook her head. 'She was a "good-time girl"—that was her reputation anyway, and it came to define her. She could never grow out of it, never shake it free. As I've got older, I've come to realise that she was living in fear, that she was afraid people wouldn't like her any more if she wasn't always the life and soul of the party.'

'I'm sorry if she lived with that fear.'

'I am too.' Amelia swallowed. 'But I spent a long time being angry with her.'

'Why?' he asked, though he had his own reasons for feeling anger towards her too.

'She shouldn't have kept me,' she said with a wry twist of her lips. 'I used to wish she'd put me up for adoption, you know.'

Sadness for the young Amelia flooded him—a surprising reaction, and not entirely welcome. 'Why were you afraid of her, then?' He reframed their conversation to her original statement.

'Because she was erratic, and almost always drunk or high. She'd invite random people back to whatever hotel we were living in at the time. I can't even tell you how often I woke up and found she'd left the hotplate on or taps running.'

Oh, *Cristo.*

Tears sparkled on Amelia's lashes, making her eyes shine like the ocean on a sun-filled day but, instead of letting them roll down her cheeks, she ground her teeth together, her expression almost mutinous. 'New boyfriends every few weeks—some of them creepy or not very nice, some of them fun but bad for her. I resented them all.' She shook her head. 'No, I hated them all. I hated them for taking her away from me. She was never a great mum, but at least when she was single, she'd try. Not very hard.' She frowned. 'Or maybe she did try hard and she just wasn't wired that way.'

And—he couldn't help himself—he reached out, pressing his hand over hers and squeezing it. 'And yet you turned out okay,' he said, the praise too faint, too light, but he wasn't sure what else he could offer.

She wrinkled her nose again and shrugged. 'I had examples of everything I didn't want to become. It was odd, growing up that way. Lots of people might think fame is aspirational, but oh, how I hated it.' She shook her head. 'Photographers going through our trash, Mum being in those gossipy magazines every time she got dumped or stumbled out of a nightclub. When I was old enough, I did my best to protect her from it, but there was only so much I could do.'

'You must have still been a child, even then.'

'Why do you say that?'

'You were only twelve when she died…'

'Yes.' She shook her head. 'But I think having a mother like mine forces you to grow up a lot sooner.'

With a visible effort to clear her thoughts, she stretched an uneven smile across her beautiful face. 'So that's my story. What of yours?'

He didn't want to stop talking about her—having opened Pandora's Box, he wanted all the secrets, all the mysteries. 'Far less interesting,' he promised.

'I doubt that.'

The waiter appeared and they ordered—a simple lunch, vegetarian for Amelia and seafood for Antonio—and then they were alone once more.

'Your mother died when you were young?' she prompted.

Antonio expelled a breath, wondering if it was impolite to discuss such a thing with a pregnant woman. 'In childbirth,' he said at length—there was no way to sugar-coat it. 'But from *very* rare complications.'

'Oh, I hadn't realised,' she said, looking away from him. 'That's awful.'

'As I said, it was extremely rare.'

'I'm not worried about myself,' she rushed to assure him, angling her face to his, and now she turned her hand upside down, capturing his and lacing their fingers together, templing them on the table.

She looked at their interwoven fingers as she spoke—it was an intoxicating contradiction—his fingers so tanned and long, hers fair and small, with the wedding ring he'd given her sparkling back at him. 'But how awful, that she never got a chance to know you. To be a mother. And she must have been so excited.'

That had him arching a brow. 'Are you excited?'

'Are you kidding?'

He laughed then. 'No. I'm curious.'

'Of *course* I'm excited!' Her free hand curved over her stomach and his eyes followed the betraying gesture with curiosity. 'Aren't you?'

It was an excellent question. At no point had he stopped to analyse his feelings. He had discovered her pregnancy and known only that he had to make her his, and that the baby would be raised a Herrera, right here in Spain.

'I'm...'

'Yes?' She blinked at him, a smile tickling the corners of her lips, as though she were trying to suppress it—and failing.

'I'm curious.'

She burst out laughing. 'That's it?'

'Well, is it going to be like you, or like me?' he said, uncharacteristically sheepish. 'A boy, a girl, tall, short, with blue eyes that shine like the Aegean? Or dark like mine?'

She sighed. 'And isn't that...exciting? I mean, we have no idea about any of this, and yet this is our baby! No matter what, they'll be part me, part you. I can't wait to meet them.'

Her excitement was contagious and he found himself nodding, trying to fathom what their baby would be like. Their food arrived and she pulled her hand from his—he regretted the separation, and wondered at that. But for weeks he'd kept his distance and then, after last night and the magic of seeing their baby's heartbeat on the screen, suddenly, he didn't want to keep his distance any longer.

'And you were close to your dad, obviously,' she murmured, bringing the conversation back to something calmer and more grounded in the present. 'I mean, the park, the puppets, football...'

'Yes,' he agreed. 'We were close. I idolised him.'

Her eyes were speculative, loaded with questions she didn't voice. She was tentative in a way he couldn't stand. They'd been sharing so much of themselves a moment ago, he didn't want her to withdraw from him again. 'You look like you wanted to ask me something,' he said softly, and her eyes widened with surprise.

She nodded gently. 'Is he...?'

'Yes,' he confirmed, unprepared for the rush of emotion that filled him. 'He's dead.' He frowned. 'Saying that is strange. I haven't...talked about him in the past tense yet.' A frown stretched across his handsome face. 'My father was an incredibly dynamic man—larger than life. I still find myself forgetting that he is gone sometimes.'

'I'm sorry.' She speared a small tomato and lifted it to her lips. 'You must miss him a lot.'

'Yes.' He reclined in his chair, taking in the view, his expression unknowingly sombre. 'When your brother set out to destroy Herrera Incorporated, it was very hard on my father. He'd spent his life building the company up, making it bigger and better than it had been under his father, and to have that in jeopardy—' He turned back to face her and for a moment he recalled she was a diSalvo, and he remembered all the reasons he had for keeping her at a distance.

But then she sighed, a soft, small noise, and she was so sympathetic that he couldn't throw her in the same box as her brother and father. She was different—lacking the killer instincts that had brought his father to his knees.

'I imagine that must have been very difficult for you.'

'Yes,' he drawled, and at her look of pain he grimaced, making an effort to soften his expression. 'The markets were weak and confidence was low. His investors deserted him—he was left with barely anything.'

'But you rebuilt it,' she said.

His nod was short.

'That must have taken an incredible amount of work.'

He shrugged laconically. 'It's what I'm good at.'

Her smile was just a shiver across her lips. 'I can see that.'

'I needed him to know that Herrera Incorporated was valuable again. It's more than a business, *hermosa*. This is a birthright. A legacy. No one wants to leave something worse than when they inherited. But my father...' he said, breaking off, not quite sure why he felt so free to confide in Amelia when he generally made a point of holding his private matters close to his chest. But she waited patiently, her enormous eyes promising him discretion, encouraging him to finish his sentence. 'He was a gentleman,' he went on, smiling as he surrendered to the memory. 'He believed in honour and decency. He came from a time when a man's handshake truly was as good as his word—and a word between decent people meant more than a contract. It was naïve, in hindsight, but it's how he'd always done business. It was easy for your brother to target him.' He cleared his throat. 'The despair almost killed him.'

She blanched visibly. 'You couldn't do anything to stop it?'

'Not at the time. My father didn't realise what was happening until it was too late. Their plan was ruthless, meticulous and executed with brilliance. Within the space of a fortnight, he'd lost almost everything.'

'I'm sorry,' she said gently, her eyes showing the sincerity of her words. 'I wish...that hadn't happened.'

How long had he been waiting for a diSalvo to apologise? A long time. But not this diSalvo—and not now. It was too late for apologies, too late for forgiveness. The die had been cast long ago: his hatred and need for vengeance had been forged in fire. No words could weaken those feelings.

'It is part of our history now,' he said, sipping his drink, his eyes holding hers.

'But not our future,' she ventured, her look one of hope.

He stayed silent—how could their future be anything but?

'When did he die?' she asked, turning the conversation away from their blood feud when he didn't respond. And he was relieved by that—another out-of-character feeling, for Antonio Herrera *never* shied away from a conflict.

'Not long ago.'

A frown flickered across her face. 'When?'

'Four months,' he said.

Her frown deepened. 'That's right before we met?'

'A month before,' he agreed.

'You didn't tell me.'

'Why would I?' he prompted, as though it didn't matter. As though his father's death hadn't invigorated his passionate need for revenge. As though it hadn't scored through his flesh like acid with new resentments, fresh pains.

'Because,' she responded with exasperation, 'we talked about stuff and because it feels like something your wife should know,' she said simply. And then, less simply, infinitely more pleasurably, 'Because I *want* to know stuff like that. Because maybe I could help you. Maybe talking is important.'

Her kindness was unexpected and touching—it was also unsettling. Because he suspected he didn't deserve kindness—particularly not from Amelia.

'Perhaps seeing you put all thoughts of my father from my mind,' he said, aiming to lighten the mood.

Her cheeks glowed pink, but she dropped her gaze, suddenly pretending fascination with the meal in front of her.

'I doubt that.'

'Do you?'

'Yes.' And she looked him square in the eyes, and something in the region of his chest tightened. 'You came to me because of your father. Why else would you act then? Shortly after his death, you enact this revenge plan of yours?'

'It wasn't that,' he said, although of course the timing had seemed fortuitous. 'It took my detective some time to locate you.'

'Detective?' she repeated, scandalised. 'You had a detective looking for me?'

His shrug was more relaxed than he felt. 'You weren't in Italy, as I'd presumed you would be. Nor were you in London. Who would have thought you'd take up a job as a teacher in a school in a town in the middle of nowhere, using an assumed name? It was as though you were trying to disappear from the face of the earth.'

Her lips twisted. 'I suppose I kind of was.' Her expression assumed a faraway look. 'I love my family, Antonio.' She sent him a look, and he heard the words she hadn't said: *Enough to marry you to save them.* 'But I never fitted into their way of life. I didn't like the sense of being a commodity rather than a person. All my life, I've wanted to be normal. Just a regular person with a real job, who can do normal things. That's why I was in tiny village in the middle of nowhere. It's why I became a teacher.'

His chest compressed at the picture she painted, of a girl always out of place and time, and he couldn't help the surge of guilt that rushed through him. Because he'd dragged her back into the spotlight, and deep down he knew she would have been happier if only he'd left her alone.

'But a detective?' she teased, turning their conversation back to his method of locating her.

He took her lead, but his mind was raking over her admission of having felt so out of place, and making a new kind of sense of that. Her refusal to take part in a wedding reception suddenly made sense, and he marvelled at his insensitivity. Her reaction had been unusually panicked. Now he understood that. Pity clouded his eyes but he kept his voice light.

'Why does that surprise you?'

'I suppose it shouldn't. You wanted my shares in Prim'Aqua; you did what you needed in an attempt to procure them—including sleuthing me out with a private eye. You don't let anything stand in the way of your dreams.'

But her words rankled and he needed to reject them instantly. 'I didn't come to your home to seduce you, Amelia,' he said throatily. 'What happened between us that night was as simple as me wanting you and you wanting me.'

'It wasn't simple,' she said softly. 'Not with all this between us.'

Never had truer words been spoken, yet still he sought to refute the statement. 'I wasn't thinking of our families when I took you to bed.'

And more heat suffused her cheeks and, *Cristo*, he wanted her in that moment. He wanted her, but not just because his body was tight with desire. He wanted her because he longed to kiss her, to make her cry out for him; he ached to seduce her slowly, to show her how it could be between two people completely in sync. Their single night together had been too short; had he known he would not have the pleasure of her company again, he would have lingered over their lovemaking, enjoying every move and thrust, every shift of their bodies in that primal heat. He would have helped her learn the ways of her own body, the pleasure she was capable of feeling, what she longed for most.

'I'm glad to hear it,' she said, but the words hitched in her throat and there was a breathless quality to them that spoke of her own desires and needs, and how he ached to indulge those!

And, despite the fact this was all new and different, and he didn't know what they were doing, he reached for her hand and lifted it to his lips, pressing a kiss against her fingertips as his eyes held hers.

Her lashes fluttered closed, but not before he saw the desire swirling in their cornflower-blue depths. Not before her lips parted on a sharp intake of breath.

Sensual heat was in the air around them, and he had no intention of ignoring it this time.

Did he have any idea what he was doing to her?

She tried to focus on the page of her book, but with Antonio doing push-ups on the terrace just beyond her, wearing a pair of black bathing briefs, his broad, tanned chest on display, his powerful legs, his dark hair slicked against his head like a pelt after his early evening swim—she was lost, powerless, completely entranced. The words in her book swirled before her eyes and she valiantly made an effort to read the paragraph once more.

It was her own fault, she supposed, for picking up *Anna Karenina*. Having read it before and suffered through a more in-depth appraisal of nineteenth-century Russian agriculture than anyone truly needed, she wasn't exactly sure why she'd felt compelled to pick it up once more.

It was hardly engrossing.

Not as engrossing as her husband, in any event. Their conversation over lunch had got deep under her skin. His insistence that he had come to her to buy shares but had then wanted *her*, not because of Prim'Aqua, not because of anything. Except desire. Lust. Need. Passion.

She hadn't realised until lunch how desperately she'd needed his assurances on that score and, now that she had them, how empowering it was. Because it legitimised what she felt—it showed that, no matter what else they were, this desire was real. It was true. He hadn't seduced her because he'd thought it would lead to her compliance. He'd been unable to resist her.

For the hundredth time in a handful of minutes, her eyes lifted towards the terrace. He wasn't looking at her. She allowed herself a moment to stare, to savour the lines of his body, the sleek, smooth masculinity that was all hard edges and beautiful planes, and then turned back to her book.

Two sentences later and her eyes lifted and finally, with an exasperated sound, she dropped the book and stood.

Did he have any idea what he was doing to her? Surely he did.

And couldn't two play at that game?

With a small smile on her lips, she slipped upstairs and

strolled into the enormous walk-in wardrobe. He'd filled it with designer clothes, but she'd assiduously ignored them, preferring to wear clothes she felt most like herself in, to wear the clothes of her old life like a uniform.

Only she hadn't brought a swimsuit with her, and she knew there were several stashed in one of the drawers. She opened the first—it was filled with jewels, so she snapped it shut and went lower. The next drawer revealed what she was looking for.

She pulled out a simple navy-blue bikini and dressed quickly, pulling her hair over one shoulder as she crossed the room on her way back downstairs. Only the sight of herself in the full-length mirror arrested her step for a moment.

She curled her hands over the hint of a curve, a smile stretching her lips from one ear to the other.

She began to walk once more, but the smile didn't shift. So as she stepped out onto the terrace she'd almost forgotten that a small part of her had wanted to go and get into a swimsuit just to repay the sensual distraction Antonio had been subjecting her to for the past hour. He was doing sit-ups now and, as he pulled towards his knees, he stopped, holding himself there, his body sheened in a light layer of perspiration so that he glistened all over, his expression burning her with its intensity. He dragged his eyes from her face, down her body, over the soft curve of her breasts to her newly rounded stomach, her legs and then back up, until her skin was covered in goosebumps and her heart was racing.

He stood slowly and, with the same pace, she took a step towards him, her eyes unable to pull away from his.

'You are…' He spoke with a voice that was husky, words that were dredged from deep inside his soul.

She held her breath, waiting for him to finish the sentence, but he shook his head, as if to clear the thought.

'Yes?' she asked breathlessly.

'You are beautiful,' he said finally and moved a hand to curve around her cheek, tilting her face towards his.

She could hardly swallow, so dry was her mouth. 'Thank you.'

'I cannot believe this.' And he dropped his hands to her stomach, discovering the roundness there for himself.

'I know; it's kind of surreal,' she said, trying to sound light and breezy.

But the look on his face rid her of any such notion. There was such an acute watchfulness in his expression, a sense of powerful, passionate possession, that she took a step closer, as close as she could get without touching him, and then he went the rest of the way, closing the gap and wrapping one arm around her waist. He held her, vice-like, to his body and she made a soft sound of surrender before his lips dropped to hers and he kissed her, his mouth demanding, as though everything was hinged on this kiss.

She tilted her head, giving him more access, and she lost herself in that moment but she found herself too.

Emotions surged inside her but Amelia couldn't have described them—not happiness, not doubt. She was a mix of everything and nothing; she knew only that answers lay within this kiss, within this touch, within him.

He lifted her easily, cradling her to his chest and carrying her towards the pool. And, despite the fact he was moving in that direction, the feel of cool water against her sun-warmed and passion-heated body still made her gasp. He swallowed the gasp and kissed it right back to her, and she laughed softly as the water rose higher and higher.

She spun in his arms, wrapping her arms around his neck and her legs around his waist, and then she kissed him with all the pent-up hormonal needs that were ravaging her common sense and making her need Antonio more in that moment than she'd ever needed anyone or anything.

'Make love to me,' she demanded, her hands weaving behind his back, interlocking and holding him tight.

He groaned, a guttural noise that was empowering to Amelia for it spoke of his desperation and slavery to this feeling, and she was so glad for that! Glad he was as lost to this as she. Glad he was as in her thrall as she was his.

'Why?' he asked, but his hands were curving around her rear, lifting her so she felt the strength of his arousal and tipped her head back. Her hair fell into the water, saturated, and he kissed the exposed column of her neck then found the tie for her bikini.

'Because you're my husband,' she said as he stripped the bikini top from her, discarding it in the water. His eyes devoured her breasts before his lips took over, his mouth moving over one of her nipples and then the next.

It wasn't a reason. At least, it wasn't as simple as being her husband: there were so many other factors. Having known this pleasure only once, she wanted to feel it again. She wanted to feel everything he could show her. She ran her hands over his body, delighting in the feel of his skin beneath her touch and the way he responded to her inquisitive exploration.

'Make love to me,' she whispered again, like an incantation, a demand that needed fulfilling, dropping her lips to his shoulder and nipping the flesh there with her teeth.

And there was a look of intense understanding in his eyes, a look of fierce determination too. 'I intend to, *querida*.'

Relief soared inside her and she found his mouth with hers, kissing him as though there was nothing between them but this passion, this heat. She kissed him as though this were a new beginning, and all the old hatreds and resentments were nowhere to be seen. In that moment, she wasn't a diSalvo and he wasn't a Herrera, and there were no storm clouds threatening on their horizon.

Her hands roamed his body in all the ways she'd been wanting to do since that night in the cottage. Movements that her dreams had crystallised became real. She pushed at his shorts, a low, keening noise in her throat when her fingertips grazed the strength of his arousal, the promise of his possession.

He pulled his head from hers, his expression one of utter need when he stared down at her. And awakening too, as though he were shifting out of a dream state and discovering this new reality.

'Why the hell haven't we done this sooner?' he demanded gruffly, finding her bikini bottoms and pushing them down at the same time she kicked out of them.

'Because we're stupid,' she said, the words intended as a joke but coming out seriously. There was nothing funny about the intensity of their desire.

'*Sí,*' he grunted, lifting her legs and staring at her for a long, intense moment before wrapping her around his body and sinking his powerful arousal deep into her moist core.

She groaned as he swept inside her, remembered sensations kicking to life along with new ones. It was so overwhelming! And as he thrust deep into her feminine centre, he brought his mouth to hers and his kiss mirrored the movements of his body, so her blood stirred to his tempo, gushing fast and desperately. She writhed in his arms, her ankles crossed behind his back, her hands tangling in the dark pelt of his hair, and then pleasure turned to something far harder to quantify—something earth-shattering and mind-blowing. She dug her nails into his back, scoring red marks over his flesh as the pleasure became unbearable and finally she exploded, holding onto him for dear life as everything she'd ever known seemed to fade into a distant, faraway pinprick of light.

She was high above the earth and there was only this—blinding, inconceivable light.

Amelia held onto him as slowly she sunk back down to earth, her eyes blinking open in disorientation to find she was in the pool, held by Antonio, his body tight against hers, his arousal still rock-hard inside her. He was watching her, and heat bloomed in her cheeks to recall what madness she'd just succumbed to. How lost she'd been to the feelings he could stir within her so easily.

But realisation didn't last long before he moved within her once more, this time watching her, their eyes locked in an ancient, primal examination. He watched as he drove himself deep inside her, he watched as her teeth sunk into her lip to stop herself from crying out, and he shook his head, lifting his thumb and rubbing it over her lips. 'Do not censor yourself.' The words were heavy with his exotic accent, thrilling over her nerve endings, setting little fires beneath her blood.

Before he could pull his hand away, she sunk her mouth around his thumb and his eyes flared wide at the sight of her pink lips swallowing a part of him.

His own groan was loud then, and power surged inside her to know that she could drive him every bit as wild as he could her. '*Tentadora,*' he growled, his strong, virile thrust sending spasms of awareness spiralling through her.

'Right back at you,' she whimpered, digging her nails into his shoulder as another wave of pleasure built.

But he stilled suddenly, his face wiped of anything she could discern, his expression unrecognisable. 'I want you to be my wife, Amelia,' he said, and the words were foreign and confusing when all she could think of was sensual pleasure.

'I am.' She rolled her hips, needing him to keep doing what he had been, needing him to keep pushing her towards the edge of what she could bear.

'No. I want you in every sense. In my bed, by my side. From now on. *Entiendes?*'

Something other than pleasure punched through her, something that set her soul on fire, that she couldn't analyse and couldn't comprehend, beyond knowing that it mattered more than the world to her.

'*Si,*' she moaned, rolling her hips once more. And, satisfied with her agreement, he gave her what she needed, his body resuming its rhythm, driving her higher and higher into the heavens. And as she stood on the precipice, preparing to dive into an unknown heaven, he was there with her, his body vibrating alongside hers, and they clung together as they fell apart, into a billion pieces of what they had once been.

CHAPTER TWELVE

ANTONIO HAD ALMOST forgotten about the interview. It had been given months ago—shortly before their wedding, when Amelia had still been, for the most part, simply a diSalvo to him. A month before they'd slept together again and formed a new kind of relationship, one that existed outside the bounds of their blood feud.

Since that day in the pool, something had shifted for them. She'd come to his bed each night and he'd slept wrapped around her, a hand possessively curved over her stomach and a certainty in his chest that she was right where she belonged.

He stared at the newspaper spread over his desk and the photo they'd chosen to print of her, and his gut twisted with a mix of fury and disgust. She was only young in this picture—ten, perhaps? And her mother stood beside her, wearing a skimpy dress and huge sunglasses, looking every bit the drugged-out supermodel he had discovered her to have been.

Perhaps if he didn't know Amelia as he did now, he wouldn't have noticed the fear in her eyes. Nor the panic stretched across her beautiful young face.

But he understood every cell in her beautiful body, he *knew* her, in many ways better than he did himself. And even though they'd met only eight months earlier, seeing her in this picture, he understood exactly what she was feeling. There were photographers in the background of the photo, paparazzi, and her small fingers were curved around her mother's, as though she were the protector, the adult.

He swore a guttural oath into his office as he reached for his phone and dialled her number on autopilot. His eyes took in the headline to the left of the article: *Tycoon's Marriage Merger!*

His gut clenched.

In a move the billionaire businessman himself describes as 'fortuitous', the marriage of Amelia diSanto to Antonio Herrera brings together two warring dynasties—and a merging of assets that will form one of the biggest financial powerhouses in the world.

*   *'Prim'Aqua will be at the heart of my business operation going forward,' Herrera says. 'It gives me great satisfaction to bring the company back into the fold. The future is bright.'*

He hadn't even been misquoted. He *had* said that, and myriad other self-congratulatory statements lauding his own success in reacquiring Prim'Aqua. At the time, he'd thought only of Carlo's reaction on reading the news. He'd taken pleasure from imagining his sworn enemy having to see evidence of Antonio's success—and the marriage that would add insult to injury.

He hadn't thought of Amelia. Not when he'd given the interview.

He hadn't *known* her then. He hadn't known that she'd wish to keep this marriage secret, to give herself time to adjust to it. He hadn't known that she would turn out to be every bit as sweet as she'd seemed that night, long ago, in Bumblebee Cottage. He hadn't known that he would come to depend on her, that she could answer every single one of his needs.

His eyes dived to the next page, where there was a photo with him and one of his ex-lovers. A woman whose name he struggled to remember in that moment. *Billionaire Bachelor!* ran the second headline, and there was a list of his famous past lovers.

His chest felt as though it were being split in two.

'Answer your phone,' he snapped, then hung up and dialled her number again.

It rung out, but he kept trying, all the while reading the article.

Every paragraph showed it to be so much worse.

Hell, he'd forgotten about this interview, because it hadn't mattered to him at the time. He'd given no thought to Amelia, and how she might feel. She'd agreed to marry him, she'd agreed to give him Prim'Aqua once their child was born, and that had been the end of it.

But now?

Dios, please let her not have seen it.

With another oath, he grabbed his suit jacket and swung his arms into it as he walked, stalking towards the door of his office and slamming it in his wake.

'Sir? You have an appointment in ten…'

'Cancel my afternoon,' he bit out, jabbing a finger against the door of the lift. 'Cancel it all.'

He barely recognised himself in the shimmery reflection of the lift. His face was white beneath his tan. So this, then, was what true fear felt like.

Amelia stirred her tea, a gentle smile on her face. She daydreamed a lot lately. And she smiled a lot too.

Her hand curved over her rounded tummy—now so big she couldn't sit in properly against a table. She could use it as a table, she thought with a grin, as she balanced a book on it just for fun.

She stifled a yawn, then looked towards the clock. It was

still the early afternoon. She'd taken to napping, to catch up on sleep, because her nights were hardly as restful as they could be. Warmth suffused her body as she remembered the way Antonio had kissed her all over the night before, his mouth finding her most intimate core and his tongue driving her beyond wild, until her nails had almost torn shreds in the silk sheets of his bed and heat had threatened to burn her from the inside out.

He knew exactly how to touch her, to kiss her, to hold her, to give her more pleasure than she could put into words.

She stood slowly, stretching her arms above her head before reaching for her tea and carrying it with her towards her bedroom.

Her phone screen was glowing when she stepped inside and she moved towards it on autopilot, scooping it up to see a screen covered in alerts.

Missed calls—lots of them. From Antonio's office phone and Carlo's mobile.

Her heart began to trip faster and faster. She hadn't spoken to Carlo in months, except via text. It had been too hard to talk to him, knowing that she was lying to him, and she still hadn't been ready to face the reality of her brother and father's outrage. And they *would* be outraged when they discovered she'd married Antonio—that she was pregnant with his baby.

She needed time—and wanted to protect the marriage that they were building. A marriage that, in her heart, she suspected couldn't have been more perfect if their meeting had been a true love match. Because she loved him with all her heart and every inch of her soul, and she suspected he felt the same.

He had to.

Love didn't exist in a vacuum. One person couldn't have enough love to create this abundance of feeling.

She skipped into the voicemail section of her phone.

None from Antonio, several from Carlo. Concern for her father came to the forefront of her mind—it would make sense that both men would try to contact her if something had happened to Giacomo.

She lifted the phone to her ear, bracing herself for whatever was to come. But she couldn't have imagined it would be anything like this.

'Amelia? What the hell is going on?'

Several curse words in Italian.

'You're pregnant? Tell me that bastardo *is not the father. I swear, I'll kill him.'*

Her skin shivered with goosebumps as she tried to make sense of how Carlo had learned the truth. She'd been so careful, and she knew Antonio understood her desire to keep their marriage quiet. So? How had Carlo learned of this?

She clicked into the next voicemail; it was even angrier.

'Call me back, damn it! What the hell is happening? You married Antonio Herrera? He'll eat you alive and spit you back out for breakfast. How could you be so stupid? The man is a bastard, capable of only hatred and revenge. He is the devil.'

The next one was just a string of angry Italian, finishing with, *'How could you do this to me? He's using you, Amelia—and, damn it, you're letting him. He's using you to get to me!'*

She was ice-cold and dropped the phone to the bed just as it began to ring anew. Carlo.

She lifted it to her ear. *'Digame.'*

'Damn it, where have you been, Millie?'

'Not near my phone,' she said, sitting down on the edge of the bed, numb.

'Well?' The word was bitten out and she swept her eyes shut. 'Is it true?'

'I…'

'You're married to him?'

'I…'

'Damn it! Do you know who he is? He hates us, Millie. How could you do this?'

'It wasn't…' She bit down on her lip and stared at her hands, her wedding ring glinting as she looked at it.

'He's using you!'

'No, it's not like that. Our marriage isn't…anything to do with this feud.'

He swore in disagreement. 'He told me he would take everything I care about and destroy it, just for the sake of it. I thought he meant my businesses; I had no clue he was speaking of my own sister. He seduced you and convinced you to marry him purely to hurt me. Can't you see that?'

'No!' She shook her head, her mind clinging to the intimacy she shared with her husband, to the truth of what they'd become.

'Yes. Do you doubt him capable of it? He who has set out to bring down our whole empire?'

'You did the same to him,' she fired at him, her stomach in knots.

'To get him to back off!' Carlo grunted. 'But this was always about him—and his ability to destroy us. His sick need to avenge a generations-old feud. This is the man you've married. Is this *bastardo* to be the father to my nephew?'

She wanted to dispute what he'd said, but memories of conversations spun into her mind—his description of his childhood, the love he'd felt for his father. A father who'd suffered as a result of Carlo's machinations.

It was all too hard to process.

'How did you find out about us?' she asked, turning to the one thing she could attempt to make sense of in that moment.

'The article,' he snarled. 'Tell me you've seen it?'

'I…no.'

'Then you are in for a wake-up call. Your *husband*—' he spat the word '—couldn't help boasting about taking over our family empire. "A perfect merger", he calls it. You are little more than an afterthought—a bride for the sake of business. *This* is the man you married.'

Her chest felt as if it were being washed with acid. Panic was curving around her, and the baby in her belly began to flip and flop in response to the adrenal surge.

'I can't believe it.'

'It's online.' There was a pause. 'There. I've sent you a link.'

'*Gracias.*'

She disconnected the call without knowing if the conversation was at an end. Her forehead was hot and clammy as she clicked into the text message link and the article expanded on her device.

Tycoon's Marriage Merger! the headline screamed.

She read the article with a growing sense of panic and a lessening ability to breathe, then stared at her phone, the whole world seemingly made of shards of a broken mirror that she had no idea how to safely traverse.

'Amelia.' She hadn't heard him come in and the sound of his voice startled her. She lifted her gaze towards him and saw the tightness in his expression. The wariness too.

'You gave an interview?' Her words were low and throaty, her sense of betrayal evident in each sore syllable.

A muscle throbbed low in his throat and she stared at it, then shifted her gaze sideways, to the corridor beyond the door. Their baby kicked against her ribs but she didn't react.

'A long time ago,' he conceded, nodding, stepping into the room but pausing when she stiffened.

'When?' She looked at him, a plea in her features.

'Before we were married,' he said. 'I had forgotten about the damned piece.'

'Don't.' She shook her head, standing, nothing making any sense any more.

'Don't what?'

'Don't lie to me. Don't act as though this wasn't all a part of your plan.'

His brows knitted together as he stared at her, then he closed the gap between them, his stride long and purposeful. 'I am sorry the article ran. I am sorry I couldn't prepare you for it. I gave the editor an earful on the drive over here,' he said with a shake of his head.

'He's just doing his job! What were you doing? Bragging to all and sundry about how clever you are to have acquired the company you've always wanted through this...*marriage merger* of ours! That's all this is for you, isn't it?'

'I have *never* used those words to describe what we are,' he contradicted fiercely. 'And you know as well as anyone that the reason I married you is for our baby, not because of Prim'Aqua.'

She recoiled as though he'd slapped her and breath burned in her lungs. She *did* know the reason they'd married, but it still hurt to be reminded of how calculated this had all been for him. 'And somewhere between my agreeing to marry you and us actually getting married, you had time to gloat to a journalist about the controlling stake in Prim'Aqua you'd scored?'

He ground his teeth together. 'It is a statement of fact, not a gloat.'

'And the hurt this article caused my family? Can you imagine how they felt, waking up to read this?'

His expression tightened, his eyes glistening black. 'I do not care what your family felt,' he said finally, coldly, and then, with a noticeable softening of his features, 'I care about you. About any hurt this stupid journalism has caused you to feel.'

She bit down on her lip and turned her back on him. 'Hurting my family does hurt me. You've known that all along.'

He was silent.

'Nothing's changed for you, has it?'

'What do you mean?' he queried from right behind her, so his breath was warm against her flesh and her stomach twisted at his nearness and the distance she felt growing between them.

'You still hate my family—even though they're a part of me, and our baby is a part of them.'

He made a growling sound of dissent. 'Everything's changed. We are married. When I gave that interview, I didn't see you as much more than a means to an end, it's true.'

She winced.

'I have never hidden my feelings about your family.'

She frowned, knowing this to be the case and still somehow finding it impossible to process. An ache began to throb, deep in her chest. Or was it more like a ticking—incessant, unstoppable, louder and louder, speeding up and echoing the frantic racing of her heart?

'What's going to happen when our baby is born?' she whispered, curling her hands over her stomach. 'And I want to take him or her to Italy to see his grandfather? Or his uncle? Are you going to resent that? Are you going to hate me being there? Are you going to refuse to come? Or will you come and fight with two of the people I care about most?'

He ground his teeth together. 'I've told you, your relationship with them has nothing to do with me.'

She shook her head painfully. 'But what of our child's relationship with them? I will be raising our baby to love their whole family—that means my family—to talk about them with love, to speak Italian and understand his or her heritage. My child will have your last name but it will still be my child, of my family, with all that implies.'

His expression was shuttered. 'But around me he will be Herrera,' Antonio said simply. 'As you are now.'

The ache in her chest grew. 'I'm not any part of this feud,' she said. 'And I can't believe you're continuing after all this!'

'I am doing no such thing,' he said, his expression sombre. 'I have made *no* move against your brother since we married. I have left his business interests alone, even though I have had opportunity to destroy him ten times over. What is this if not proof that I am standing by our agreement?'

'Our agreement?' She paled. 'That's why you've backed off from Carlo's companies?'

He spun her around in his arms, his eyes searching hers. 'Why else?' The question was asked as if from the depths of his soul, as though he truly couldn't comprehend what was wrong with that statement. 'I am doing what you asked of me.'

And suddenly she needed to sit down. She collapsed onto the edge of the bed, pressing her fingertips into her temples.

'*Hermosa*, what is it?'

She ignored his apparent concern. 'That damned deal we made way back then is why you've left Carlo alone? You've let him be only because I'm giving you Prim'Aqua.' Her eyes glistened when she lifted them to his. 'That's all you care about.'

He swore softly. 'Not all I care about.'

'Yeah?' she demanded, scoffing.

'You know I care about you. It is why I'm here, Amelia, in the middle of the afternoon. Because the thought of you reading that article and thinking I had just given this interview...'

'But you don't love me,' she interrupted curtly, gnawing on her lower lip.

His eyes showed consternation when they locked to hers, impatience too. 'Love is beside the point,' he intoned flatly, and the words seemed to come from a long way away. 'I respect you and value you. I desire you and I have chosen to make a life with you.'

'But *love* would be a reason to leave my family alone. Love would be a reason for you to forget your hatred of them.'

'Nothing will allow me to do that,' he said gently, crouching down so his eyes were level with hers. 'I have hated them for ever and, no matter what role you play in my life, I can't simply forget how I feel.'

'You strike me as a man who can do anything he wants. So what you're saying is that you don't *want* to forgive them.'

His jaw was square, and the room was heavy with angst and sorrow for a moment before he nodded curtly. 'No,' he said at length. 'I do not want to forgive them. I want to hate them. I like hating them.'

'Even when it hurts me.'

He shook his head curtly. 'They are separate to us.'

'No, they're not.'

'They have to be. For our child, we must separate your family…'

'No, for our child, you must forget your need for revenge…'

'No.' A simple, final word that was like a nail in the coffin of all of her hopes.

'So your hatred for them is greater than anything you feel for me,' she said with a nod, as the truth of their relationship crystallised in her mind. 'You still expect me to hand over my shares in Prim'Aqua when our child is born?'

A muscle jerked in the base of his jaw and he didn't answer for a beat. Then, 'It's what we agreed.'

Her throat thickened with the threat of tears—tears she

refused to let fall. 'And you'll take Prim'Aqua to devastate Carlo? You'll take it and you'll use me to hurt him. Yes?'

He didn't answer and, quite demented by her grief, she stood and shoved at his chest, her hair whipping her cheeks as she pushed him. And he stayed where he was, impenetrable and strong, and then finally he tilted his head, just a tiny movement.

'Yes.'

Silence fell, condemnatory and grief-laced.

'And you can't even see how wrong that is, can you?'

Antonio gripped her wrists, holding her hands still against his chest. Her words were like blades in his side. 'I want Prim'Aqua,' he said, as though it were simple. He didn't need to be looking at his wife to know she was close to tears. He heard it in her voice, when she spoke next.

'More than you want me?'

'I want you both,' he said finally. 'I want you, I want this baby. And, yes, I want Prim'Aqua. That was our agreement.'

'I know that.' Her voice sounded husky, scored by sadness. 'But we were different people six months ago. I thought we were going to try to make this marriage real—'

'In what way is it not?' he interrupted, wishing he hadn't turned to look at her when he was confronted with such obvious despair on her features.

'There's no love here,' she said simply. 'Not from you.'

Her words filtered through his brain and something like an alarm bell sounded. 'Are you saying you've fallen in love with me?' he asked, incredulous, surprised, and not sure what else.

'Yes.' It was a simple answer, one that made his heart jump and panic all at once. 'I love you,' she said, and there was a part of him that rejoiced at that, and a larger part that wanted her to take the words back because they were undeserved and unasked for. Because they complicated a situation that should have been straightforward—an agreement between two parties, just like he was used to. 'But I can't do this.'

'Do what?'

'You can't actually think this marriage will work, with you hating my brother like this? With you intent on destroying him, determined to hold onto your revenge and your anger and your hatred. Not if there's a chance you're going to poison my child against him.'

The bottom was falling out of Antonio's world. Her words might as well have been spoken in Swahili for all the sense they made. There were very few facts in life he knew for certain, and one of those was that the diSalvo and Herrera families were enemies, to the death. He had no compassion for Carlo, no room for forgiveness for Giacomo. They deserved whatever fate he could conspire to give them.

And Amelia? What of her pain and hurt?

He faced the prospect of Amelia walking away from him and he wanted to assume super-human form, to build a wall as high as the sun to keep her in his home. To trap her? *Dios*, had he not already done that with this marriage?

Apparently not, if she was threatening to leave him. 'Your reasons for being married to me haven't changed,' he pointed out, falling back on his skills as a negotiator to silence the panicked drumming of his heart. 'We want the same things for our child—'

'No, we don't.' She fixed him with a level stare, icy determination in her own eyes now. 'I want my kids to have what I never did. I don't want them to live with uncertainty and insecurity, doubt, and a lack of love. And I'm sure as heck not prepared to bring my child into a war zone.'

Her words cut him to the core. 'You and I aren't a war zone! Look at how well things work between us!'

She sucked in a shallow breath. 'Because we haven't been tested! We work because we've existed as an island, totally separate from the reality of our situation. But we can't raise our child in a void! I won't deny them their heritage, and the love they can know from my family. You have no one left—no parents, no siblings, nothing you can offer them by way of an extended family. Carlo and Giacomo are it.'

'Better to have no family than those two *bastardos*—'

Her eyes fluttered shut, her lashes two dark fans against her pale cheeks. 'I can't accept that,'

'You have already accepted it,' he pointed out softly. 'You married me and you knew how I felt, and what I wanted. Carlo was bound to find out about us at some point, so now he knows. This is not the end of the world.'

She made a scoffing noise. 'He's *devastated*. He thinks you're using me to avenge your father. He thinks our marriage is just the next step in your revenge plan.' Her skin paled visibly. 'And the worst thing is, he's right.'

'Madre de Dios, you cannot actually believe this is all about revenge.'

'Not all of it, no,' she conceded softly. 'But it's a part of our marriage, and it shouldn't be.'

He ignored the compulsion to point out that their marriage *had* been born out of a desire for revenge—the words were lodged inside him, yet he couldn't speak them.

'Our marriage is immune from this.'

Scepticism showed in her expression. 'So you're telling me I can walk away from you without consequence? That you'll let me go and not set out to destroy Carlo?'

He ground his teeth as he processed her request and finally shook his head. 'No. The only thing stopping me from eviscerating him is you.'

'No, not me,' she said flatly. 'The fact I'm willing to go along with this charade.'

'You just said you love me,' he responded tautly, ignoring the throbbing deep in his chest. 'How can you then call our marriage a charade?'

'Because love doesn't exist in a black hole. My love means nothing without yours in return.'

His eyes sparked with hers but he didn't give her what she needed—and his words would have been meaningless, in any event. Meaningless when he was showing her with his actions how little he cared for her.

Sadness for the path he was set upon curdled her blood. 'Can't you see that you're pursuing revenge even when it's destroying your life? You are letting this feud become the whale to your Ahab.'

His eyes locked to hers and his chest felt as though a slab of bricks had been laid over it. 'I am doing what is needed.'

She hissed like a cat in an alley. 'Don't be ridiculous! To what? Avenge your father? I'm sorry, Antonio, but he's dead.' She winced apologetically. 'And I don't think he'd want you to use his death as an excuse to ruin your life. I don't think he'd want you to destroy your marriage in his name.'

He straightened his shoulders, staring at her down the bridge of his nose, nostrils flaring with his attempt to stay calm. She was his wife, but now she was taking it too far. 'You do not know anything about him.'

'I know that he was a man who took you to the park on weekends. Who cleared his schedule to read you books, to play with you. I know that he was a man who loved you and wanted you to be happy. Don't you owe it to him to try to move on from this?'

A beat of silence passed, heavy with her words, her hopes, his darkness. And then he spoke clearly, coldly and with finality. 'I am doing this *for* my father. I promised myself I would make Carlo pay for what he did and now I have the means of doing so. Do you think this won't make me happy?'

She took a step back, her expression like a wounded animal.

'Even when that means I'll leave?'

He stared at her, his eyes roaming her face, and then he shrugged—he appeared so cold, so measured, when his insides were shredding. 'If you truly love me, then you will understand what motivates me. You will accept this anger is a part of me, and you won't seek to change me.'

'I want to help you!' she denied hotly. 'No one should live their life with so much hatred. This is so pointless! So futile! I'm not saying you and Carlo should become best friends, heaven forbid, but can't you at least try to put the past in the past?'

'It is a part of who I am,' he said simply. 'As sure as I have two arms and legs, hating him is in my soul.'

'And loving him is in mine. I won't have my child be torn between us—feeling as though he's betraying you because he adores his uncle.'

'I've told you, I have no intention of letting our child be caught up in this.'

'How can you possibly prevent it?' She didn't wait for an answer . 'And what of me? You said last night you'd never do anything that would upset me. Can't you see how this is pulling me apart?'

A muscle spasmed low in his jaw. 'Have I spoken to you of your brother since we married? Have I brought up our feud, even once?'

She blinked, her expression one of bafflement. 'You haven't needed to! It's been in every conversation with us, every day! Why do you think I never speak of them?'

'Because they are nothing to us!'

She ground her teeth together. 'It's my *father*. He took me in when I was completely alone—'

'And you were miserable with him! That's why you hid away in that tiny village…'

'Yes, I wanted a different life, but that doesn't mean I don't love them!' She closed her eyes for a moment, sucked in a breath, hoping it would breathe strength into her. 'It doesn't mean I'll let you destroy them.'

His eyes narrowed and the threat she was making struck something in his chest, like a match to petrol. 'I don't need your permission.'

'You need my shares,' she pointed out.

'No. I have enough to ruin him, remember? To make him crumble into nothingness. Prim'Aqua is my first preference, but without it I will still succeed, *querida*.'

'Don't you dare call me that,' she spat. 'Not when you can be so ruthless and vile.'

His face flashed with surprise at her insults, and when she pressed her palm to her stomach, his eyes dropped to the gesture.

'I can't do this.' She reached for her wedding band and slid it off her finger, then her engagement ring—that had belonged to his grandmother. She held them out to him but he refused to take them, so she placed them on the table instead.

'I can't be your wife, I can't raise this baby with you, and I can't give you Prim'Aqua.' Her voice cracked. 'Our deal's off, Antonio. Destroy him if you will, but know that I will never, ever be able to forgive you if you do. Know that you will turn my love to hatred. It's your decision.'

CHAPTER THIRTEEN

HE SWORE UNDER his breath, watching as she disappeared into the wardrobe of their room. The last few minutes seemed like a dream—he could barely believe she was threatening to end their marriage.

She was upset, her shoulders shifting with silent tears, and his gut twisted with the knowledge that he'd done that to her. He'd hurt her, he'd brought her into something she hadn't even known existed.

But why? Why had this feud torn him apart, fuelled Carlo's actions, and yet Amelia had known nothing of it? Was it simply that she'd shown no interest in the business side of her family? Or was there something more to it? How could she fail to see how deep these wounds ran?

Her face, when she'd told him she was leaving, had been so full of certainty, resignation, as though that was the end of it. As though he wouldn't be able to change her mind.

That thought alone galvanised him into action—he couldn't accept the finality of that. He pushed his legs forward, carrying himself towards her, pushing into the large dressing room to find her taking clothes from drawers and laying them in a duffel bag.

And he groaned because, no matter what he felt for her family, he didn't want to lose her.

'Don't go,' he said simply, moving towards her and wrapping his arms around her waist. She swallowed a sob then, and it was a sound that tore him apart.

'Why should I stay?' she asked after a moment, pulling

away and looking at him with a challenge. She reached behind her for another stack of shirts and pushed them into the bag.

'Because you're my wife,' he said, as though it were simple.

'Yes. And I love you.' She nodded, but it was clear she didn't welcome that fact. 'But I have a track record of loving people when they can't love me back. And it destroys me—just like it did with my mother. If I stay, and pour all of myself into this marriage and our family, knowing you will never be able to give me what I need, then I'll be broken. And I won't be broken again.'

Her words landed against him like bricks. He stared at her, with no idea what he could say to change her mind.

'Tell me you love me,' she said softly, her eyes challenging him. 'Tell me you love me enough to forget your hatred for Carlo. Tell me you love me enough to leave the past alone and concentrate on our future instead.'

Silence. Her words were foreign, dipped in arsenic. He couldn't, wouldn't, soften in his resolve to destroy her brother. Never. Not even with his dying breath.

There had to be another way to get through to her. He reached for her gently, bringing her to him, and kissed her, intending to seduce her into seeing sense—or at least dependence. But he tasted her salty tears in his mouth and wrenched himself away, spinning on his heel and stalking across the dressing room.

That wasn't right either.

'I want you to stay,' he said simply, the words torn from him.

'Not enough.' She slid her feet into shoes and looked around for her handbag. She was tired—she wore no makeup and her skin was so pale, her eyes red from the sting of tears. 'And I won't stay for what you're offering.' She looked so incredibly haunted, so miserable yet so brave as she glared at him with every appearance of strength and determination, that the heart in his chest splintered apart, shattering into thousands of pieces.

'Stay because you want to,' he said softly.

She recoiled as though he'd physically hit her and his chest heaved.

'Please, stay.'

But she shook her head, and bit down on her lip. Her hands pressed to her stomach, and she moved towards the door. 'I'll let you know, when... I'll message you.'

The idea of hearing about the birth of his child through a text message sliced through his soul. How could he possibly bear to be distant from such an event? How could he be on the outside—not knowing how her delivery was going, not knowing that she was okay, that she was well?

He shook his head, opened his mouth to tell her that wasn't good enough, but she was gone, and he couldn't find any words.

What could he possibly say that would change her mind? Nothing.

And so he let her go, when it was the very last thing he wanted.

When it felt as though he were being beaten over the head. He let her go because he knew it would be best for her. And she deserved that.

Three days later and he hadn't acted. He held the shares in his portfolio and the ability to crush Carlo, and yet he still hadn't dropped the axe. Renowned for his ruthless instincts, he was hesitating at the final hurdle of a plan that he'd formed long ago. Long before he'd even met Amelia and seen her smile.

And the reason was simple.

Every time he imagined the crushing destruction of diSalvo Industries, instead of the rush of jubilation he'd expected, he felt only pain. Pain at how Amelia would respond, at how she'd judge him. Pain at how it would be the death knell to any future with her and their child.

And so he waited, and he wondered about her.

He didn't go to work. He had no interest in his office. Instead, he stalked through his home, seeing her in every room, the memories—though happy—slicing through him with their perfection. She had been everywhere, taken over everything, so that after such a short time he felt her absence completely.

The fresh flowers she had arranged in every room were beginning to wilt—that never happened while she was in the house. She always changed them before they could grow limp.

Antonio was a man who had rebuilt his crumbling family empire from the ground up; he didn't take defeat easily. But this pain was unlike any he had ever encountered.

He had failed in the one thing that mattered to him almost as much as destroying the diSalvos. He had wanted to be a good father, a great husband, yet he'd driven his wife away.

He closed his eyes and tried to picture her in Bumblebee Cottage, imagined her with all those fairy lights and her pregnant stomach, and he cursed loud and clear into the emptiness of their home. Outside, a bleak winter's day threatened rain, just like that first night he'd gone to Amelia, back in England. Only then he'd been so sure of himself, sure of his plan of attack.

Now? He knew only one thing with certainty: he couldn't let this be the end of it. He couldn't accept that their marriage was over.

Amelia would have liked to stay in bed all day, every day. She would have liked to ignore the demands of her body, to refuse to eat, to sob until her broken heart finally grieved and became light again.

Were it not for the baby inside her hugely rounded stomach, she would have indulged every single maudlin fantasy and abandoned herself completely to the grief that had saturated her soul.

She would have wept until her tear ducts dried up and her throat was red raw.

Only for her baby did she give up on self-indulgent mourning. For their baby, on a cold yet sunny winter's day, she forced herself to eat a piece of toast and a banana, to sip a cup of tea and then to dress warmly so she could go for a walk.

A small walk, she promised herself, and then she could go back to bed. Curl up as though the day weren't happening, and ignore the fact that in a matter of weeks she would have a baby, and would have to face the rest of her life without Antonio.

Her heart gave a painful squeeze as his image floated into her mind and she gasped audibly, hating how much she missed him. Hating how tempted she was to throw caution and common sense to the wind and return to Madrid, tail between her legs, pride in tatters, and tell him she would take him—on whatever terms he offered.

But she couldn't do that.

She weaved down a lane, reaching above her and grabbing a twig of jasmine as she went, lifting it to her nose and smelling it, the fragrance so perfectly intoxicating that the ghost of a smile crossed her face.

Not for long, though. Sadness and bleakness were back and she dropped the flower a few steps further.

It was colder than she'd realised and her face was icy, despite the winter sunshine. After a couple of miles, she turned back towards her cottage, already relishing the idea of being back in bed and blotting out this world for a while longer.

A sudden movement when she approached her house caught her eye and she squinted, wondering if she were hallucinating.

A man at her door looked almost exactly like… Antonio. She breathed in sharply just as he pulled his body from the door and then slammed himself against it, in an attempt to break through the ancient timber.

'Antonio!' she said sharply, moving up the small path towards the front door. 'What are you doing?'

'*Dios mío*, you are okay?'

'Of course I'm okay. Why wouldn't I be?'

If anything, he looked indignant, and as though he were controlling a temper. 'Because you weren't answering your door or your phone, and yet your car is here.'

She frowned. 'I went for a walk.'

Consternation creased his brow. 'In this condition?'

'My legs work fine,' she said softly.

'I was concerned,' he explained.

She struggled not to react. Not to let her heart throb hopefully, not to let her pulse fire. It had only been a week, but it might as well have been three years, for how desperately she wanted to stare at him and touch him. Fresh pain perforated her heart, because she couldn't give in to those feelings. He was wrong for her, wrong in every way. His hatred would poison their baby—and enough had been lost to the ancient feud. She was done.

'I could have just been ignoring you, you know,' she pointed out with a coldness she was proud of.

'I worried you could be passed out inside,' he said, and she saw for the first time that his skin was pale, as though he'd been shocked. Worried.

She forced her heart not to register that.

She was pregnant with his child; concern was natural.

'I wasn't.'

She moved to the door but he put a hand out, just lightly, brushing her forearm. 'I need to speak with you.'

Her eyes swept shut at this and she shook her head instinctively. Her voice shook when she spoke. 'I feel like we've said everything that needs saying.'

'You have,' he agreed, dropping his hand. 'But I have some way to go. I want to fix this, Amelia. If you'll let me.'

She shook her head again and lifted her fingertips to her lips, and then she took another step backwards, almost as though she were afraid of him. 'Not everything can be fixed.'

Antonio acknowledged her statement, and the truth behind it. He *couldn't* fix everything. Sometimes things were broken beyond repair and whenever he looked back on that last day in Madrid he saw the fractures he had forced into their relationship.

'I can try.' His voice was gravelly.

She turned to look at him, huge blue eyes in a face that he knew so very well. 'You shouldn't be here.'

She was pulling away from him, building up to telling him to get the hell out of her life. He had to make every word count.

'I've just come from Carlo's.'

And she paled, gasping and lifting her hands to cover her mouth. 'Oh, Antonio, *no*. What did you do?'

She was clearly terrified of him setting his plan in action—of what he might say or do to the brother she obviously loved. He'd done this to her—he'd made her think destruction was all he cared about. Wasn't that true? Destruction at any cost—and he could clearly see the cost his need for revenge had inflicted on the woman he'd married.

Shame at his actions threatened to suffocate him.

'He and I have come to an agreement.'

This she wasn't expecting. 'What kind of agreement?' Her eyes narrowed and he felt a wave of animosity bounce off her. 'Have you blackmailed him in some way? Or are you here to offer me a fresh bribe?'

'I'm here to offer you my heart.' He waited for the words to sink in. 'And to beg you to forgive me, Amelia, *querida*.' She swallowed, her neck knotting visibly. He fought an urge to reach out to her, to touch her, to comfort her in some way. 'I had been angry for so long, it was all I knew. I didn't realise I could feel any other way, until I lost you. You walked out of my life and I was filled with this huge ache, right here.'

He pushed his hand into his chest. 'I was alone and lonely for the first time in my life—and all the hatred I felt towards your family, my need to make them pay for what they did to my father, *Dios mío*, it seems so petty now. That I was willing to sacrifice our happiness to an ancient feud... That I laid my actions at my father's feet, when you were so right about him: the last thing he would have wanted would be for me to push you away.'

She swallowed, the slender column of her neck moving visibly, her chest inflating and deflating at speed. And then, after a moment, with a tiny shake of her head, 'I'm not giving you my stake in Prim'Aqua, no matter what you say.'

He couldn't blame her for believing that was all he was after, but her suspicion ripped through him nonetheless, tearing a hole in his chest. 'Good. I no longer want it.'

Her eyes showed her disbelief.

'Your brother and I have agreed to put our shares in trust—for our baby.'

At this, Amelia drew in a small, sharp breath. Surprise crossed her face. 'Why?'

'It's their birthright. It should pass to them in one piece.'

'Yes, of course.' She nodded slowly. 'I'll do the same.'

And then with another soft sigh, 'I only wish you'd thought of that right at the beginning.'

'It wouldn't have been enough,' he muttered, regretting his own stupidity. 'I wanted to destroy your brother, and nothing else would do. Not then.'

She bristled, visibly rejecting him. 'And now?'

'I no longer wish to destroy him, *hermosa*.'

Her expression showed wariness. 'Why not?'

'Because he is your brother, and you love him, and he will be the uncle to our child, just like you said. But it's more than that. I want, more than anything, to make you happy.'

She crossed her arms, the gesture one of scepticism and disbelief. 'Why are you saying this now?'

But she was tired, her skin pale. 'Come inside. Sit down,' he urged softly.

'No.' She was resolute. 'Why now? What happened?'

'You went away,' he said simply, but the words were punctuated by gravelled pain. 'And I saw everything clearly for the first time in a long time. Without you, nothing matters. It's that simple. Everything I was fighting for—to avenge a historic wrong—seemed so trivial. I just wanted you. To hold you and wake up with you, to make you smile and fetch you tea.' He stroked his thumb across her cheek, and she watched him as he studied her. 'I just want you back, so badly. I thought ours was a marriage of convenience and common sense—I had no idea until you left that I had become addicted to you—to all of you. I didn't realise that I had fallen completely in love with you.'

She was silent, her beautiful face pinched as his words settled around them, and he waited, even when anxiety was ripping him apart from the inside out.

'I don't know if you're capable of feeling love.'

The accusation hurt, but she had every reason to feel that

way, he acknowledged. Panic flared in his gut because he'd lost her once and he couldn't lose her again.

'I loved you, I think, even on that first night, when you threatened me with a meat cleaver. When you confounded all my expectations. When you made me laugh and look beyond my own stupid prejudices. When you gave yourself to me so sweetly, so willingly, and with all of the generosity that is so much a part of you.'

Tears filled her eyes and, God, he wanted them gone! He never wanted her to cry again, unless from sheer joy.

'You used me that night, Antonio. And you've been using me ever since.'

'No.' He shook his head emphatically. 'Our families had nothing to do with why I wanted you—they never did.'

'You blackmailed me into marriage—'

'I know that,' he interrupted gruffly, ripping his hand through his hair so it spiked at odd angles. 'I have been a bastard to you and I hate myself for that. I hate everything I have done to you, and yet I cannot say with confidence that I would not do it all again. I fell in love with a woman I wished I hated, and I have spent the last eight months pushing you away rather than face the fact that you're everything I've ever wanted in this life.'

Her eyes held his for a brief second before flitting away, and the sadness in them was enough to make him crumble. 'I don't deserve another chance with you, Amelia, but I am begging you for one.'

Her sharp intake of breath showed that he was hurting her and yet he couldn't stop.

'I want you to come home, to be my wife, to live with me again. I want to hold you in my arms as you sleep, to run my fingers over your hair and wrap my arms around your body. I want to kiss you every morning and make love to you every night. But I know that is a fantasy now.' He cupped her face, desperate for her to look at him, but she kept her eyes averted, staring at their feet. 'So please let me stay here, with you. In a spare room, on the sofa, anything. Let me in, just a little, so that I can show you I'm willing to work at this, that I'm prepared to be everything you could ever want. Our marriage was all on my terms— and now it can be all on yours. Just please, do not send me away, Amelia. I am begging you...'

Amelia shook her head and stepped backwards, moving away from him a little, but at least now she looked at him. Her expression was guarded; it was impossible to know what she was thinking and feeling. He waited, knowing he'd said his piece, knowing this decision was hers now, and that he had to respect her wishes.

'Why are you here?'

The question surprised him.

'Because I love you.'

Her eyes swept shut. 'But why now?'

'Because I missed you.'

'But that's not enough,' she said, and now she sobbed, and his gut twisted. 'I've been missing you too, like crazy. Walking out on you was the hardest thing I've ever done. Our marriage was just a fantasy, Antonio. There's nothing here but revenge and hatred, and a baby. If I hadn't fallen pregnant, you would never have come looking for me, right?'

'And do you know how much I hate that? Do you know how terrifying that is? I cannot imagine my life without you, not for even one more day. Call it fate or destiny, for whatever reason this child was conceived, I thank every star in the heavens.'

'A baby isn't enough to make a marriage work.'

'Our marriage,' he said, taking a step closer and curling his hand behind her neck, holding her face towards his, 'works.' And he brushed his lips over hers, almost groaning at the taste of her, the familiar feel of her.

And she swayed against him, her body softening, and he kissed her again, relishing this—the familiar, the perfection. 'Remember everything we are, everything good we have shared, and ignore this bitterness of mine towards your family. That is the future I promise you, *querida*. From this day forward, there is no anger, no resentment, no hatred. Our child is a Herrera and a diSalvo, and we are family.'

She sobbed into his mouth and he swallowed it, and kissed her deeper, harder, with all the urgency he felt in his chest, clawing at him, ripping him to pieces.

And when she pulled away it was as though he were drowning, and everything was dark and he was panicked, until she smiled and the sun burst into his life once more.

'I don't want to stay here,' she said, and she brought her lips to his and kissed him and his heart exploded with the perfection of that moment. 'Take me home, please.'

'To Madrid?'

'To our future.'

He stooped down and lifted her up, holding her against his chest as he moved back towards his car. He walked away from a home that had, that night, been wrapped in rain and storm clouds and was now bathed in milky afternoon sunshine.

And he smiled against her lips, because he had all he could ever want in life—and it was only going to get better.

EPILOGUE

'*YOU'RE* CARRYING THE next baby!' she groaned, squeezing his hand so hard he could almost feel bones crunching.

He laughed softly. 'You said that last time.'

'And I was right!'

'You're almost there,' the doctor promised. 'One last—'

'*Puuuuuuush!*' Amelia finished, a primal, guttural word. And then she collapsed back as a baby's cry sounded.

'Well?' Antonio asked, impatient. 'What is our son to have? A sister or a brother?'

'On your way to a soccer team,' she whispered, like her normal self now, a weak smile on her face.

'It's a girl.' The doctor grinned. 'And she's got quite a kick already.'

'A girl?'

Antonio smiled down at his wife, emotions surging through him. 'A little version of you.'

She grinned, holding her hands out for the baby. 'Javier won't be happy. He was desperate for a little brother.' And then tears sparkled on her lashes as she held her daughter, seeing her shock of black hair and honey skin.

'Maybe next time,' Antonio teased.

Amelia looked daggers at him. 'Next time? Unless you really are going to become a marvel of modern medicine and be the pregnant one, then let's not talk about "next time" right now.'

'But why not? When we make such perfect babies?'

He smiled at his wife, and then at their daughter.

'She is divine.' Amelia sighed. 'Just perfect.'

'Just like her mother.'

'Will you text my family?'

Antonio nodded. Giacomo and Carlo had been eagerly awaiting news of the new Herrera—strange that he rarely thought now of the feud that had first brought him to his wife's door.

So much water had flowed under the bridge since that night—so many good memories had overwritten all the bad.

And it was a truth, he decided, that it was impossible to dislike anyone who adored your children from the bottom of their heart—and there was no doubt in his mind that the diSalvo men loved this new generation of Herreras.

'I'll let them know,' he agreed. 'Soon. But for now, let's enjoy this time with our little princess.'

'Your wish is my command,' Amelia agreed softly.

'I think that's the other way around.'

'Yes, perhaps you're right.' She stifled a yawn, and love, pride and fierce adoration burst through him.

'I'm always right.' He grinned, but there was a serious note underneath, because he very nearly hadn't been.

At one time he'd almost made the biggest mistake of his life and let this woman walk out on him.

And he'd never be so foolish ever again.

He intended to do everything in his power to live happily ever after—with the love of his life and the family they'd made.

And because he was Antonio Herrera and he always got what he wanted, they did.

* * * * *

MILLS & BOON

Coming next month

CLAIMED FOR THE SHEIKH'S SHOCK SON
Carol Marinelli

Khalid had kept his word, Aubrey realised. It had been dinner, that was all.

Except she didn't want it to be all.

It was Aubrey who wanted more and, despite what he thought her to be, it was everything else that he was—strong, sensual—that somehow made her feel safe.

Some day in the future Aubrey would know her first, and it was something she had silently dreaded.

Until now.

He could never imagine the wrestle that took place in her as they walked past the bar. Khalid could not know she was a virgin and how new this all felt to her.

All he responded to was the sensual air that surrounded them. 'I'll let the desk know now and then you can call for the driver whenever you are ready. Or,' he added, for he could resist her no more, 'you can come back to my suite.'

Aubrey stopped walking and as the sun returned to the night sky, she turned to face Khalid. Aubrey had never so completely met another's gaze before. If anything, she did her level best not to catch men's eyes, yet she held his, totally.

She saw the flecks of gold and the dark rim that seemed to hold inside it a circle of fire and he neither looked nor backed away from his invitation.

'I'd like that,' Aubrey said, for it was the truth. She wanted to be with Khalid, even if just for a night. She wanted him to be her first, yet he considered her way more experienced than she was. And if she told him her truth? Aubrey was rather certain that Khalid would politely wish her goodnight.

And so she lied by omission and chose not to tell Khalid her truth, and as he moved in to kiss her, his eyes still did not look away. Aubrey could feel the warmth of his mouth even before their lips had met and both closed their eyes as they did, for there could be no other way to sample such exquisite bliss. He kissed her so lightly that if she opened her eyes Aubrey was scared that he might have disappeared. That he might be a dream. Yet his lips pressed a little more firmly and parted hers.

Aubrey had truly never known a kiss, but even with nothing to compare it to she knew that his kiss was pure bliss. She could not have fathomed how, with such a gentle touch, her heart might tumble. It was as if he had found the weak spot within, the fracture line that, correctly tapped, might shatter her.

And he felt it too.

Tonight Khalid did not want the meaningless sex he survived on. He wanted to touch and to feel and for one night to fully indulge that. Today had been exceptionally hard—new grief and the resurgence of old grief had combined—but now there was a sweet reprieve and Audrey was the one he had found it with. She had consumed him on sight and it was a relief to finally hold her in his arms and kiss her lips as he wanted to.

But then he removed his kiss, and his hands held her hips as he made sure that Aubrey was clear as to the nature of his invitation.

'You understand that you won't be sleeping in the guest room?'

Oh, she did. Her lips ached for his and Khalid's hands on her hips were necessary for they held hers slightly back and prevented them from melding into his, as they felt inclined to do, and so she answered him honestly. 'I do.'

'Then come to bed.'

Continue reading
CLAIMED FOR THE SHEIKH'S SHOCK SON
Carol Marinelli

Available next month
www.millsandboon.co.uk

COMING SOON!

We really hope you enjoyed reading this book. If you're looking for more romance, be sure to head to the shops when new books are available on

Thursday 4th April

To see which titles are coming soon, please visit

millsandboon.co.uk/nextmonth

LET'S TALK

For exclusive extracts, competitions
and special offers, find us online: